HOUSE

OF

SKYE

BY: CHRIS DIAS

Dias Ex Machina Publishing

Chris Dias
Dias Ex Machina
129 – 6807 Westgate Ave
Prince George, British Columbia
V2N 5P8
DiasExMachina@gmail.com

Written by Chris Dias

House of Skye

Front Cover / Back Cover / Spine by: Bo Dannefaer

A FAIRY TALE

ONE

I mixed in a dab of cobalt turquoise with cerulean blue. It turned the water a slight greenish hue. Before finishing the work, I shaded the gold-plated horizon with slices of burnt sienna; this process shifted the image from sunset to late evening. I had watered down zinc white, gathered it with a toothbrush, rolled my index finger across the bristles, and sprinkled a mist of stars across a blend of raw umbar and carbon black.

"It's a real place?" the receptionist asked, admiring the result hanging on the wall.

I nodded. *No fakescapes.* That was the first rule.

The receptionist's eyes occasionally moved over me as she feigned attention to the work. I didn't know if that meant interest in me or indifference in the work. I faked apathy, probably too well.

"It's a rendering of the Seven Sisters Waterfall in Norway," I said.

"Ahh," she replied. "So, what's the piece called?"

"The Seven Sisters Waterfall in Norway."

The landscape found its home in the local police department. It hung on a wall across from and in view of the holding area. Above was a sign that read, "Wish you were here." I assumed the police department's superintendent was either ignorant or malicious.

"There's no signature," she said.

"It's small, covered by the frame. Most buyers prefer modesty in their painters," I lied. Considering where the result was destined to hang, I felt it appropriate to remain anonymous. At least if she encouraged me that would have been my answer. Truthfully, the work was not worth a name.

Like me, she was only a few years out of high school and had likely never left town. She didn't catch the minor details I was proud of. Upon consideration, I felt the base of the waterfall could use some polish. I could have accented the foam as the water broke across the jutting rocks before rolling casually into the Geirangerfjord.

The photo had a boat; I didn't add it——*no marks of man* was another rule. I offered her a smile before retrieving my nylon and leather carrying case. "It's been a pleasure."

"Superintendant was thinking of another in the coffee room. Something…inexpensive."

I held the door open with my boot. "I've got a shot of the Longsheng Rice Terraces of China. It was meant for Highland Dental before they went under. Could give it up for cheap."

"What's that one called?" she teased.

I forced a smile as I made my exit. "Call me if you're interested. I'm motivated."

I worried as I left that the last statement might have come out wrong.

*

I stared blankly at the sweat-stained, overweight mother standing with me in front of the wall of paint samples. There were hundreds of shades; each had two names, none of them an actual color. An orange Home Depot apron hung from my neck.

"Oh I like this one," the customer beamed, studying the sample sheet she pulled from the wall.

I knew every shade by memory. "That's Night Shade," I answered. "It's...It's not bad. Now, what carpet did you say you had?"

"Soft Lagoon," she answered.

"I know that one, very gray. No blue, though. This has a blue tone."

"No it doesn't," she replied unpleasantly.

That happened a lot. I pointed at the paper firmly. "Yes...yes it does. It may not look like it, but there's a blue tinge. It'll jump out on your wall. It's also really dark." I fished through the other samples. "It's recommended that your carpet be a darker tone than your walls. I would go with--" I pulled out another sample-- "The Dark Granite. It's brighter. It'll offset the darker tone of the carpet."

"Well, I trust my eyes more than a teenager's," she answered. "I'll take the Night Shade."

I paused to consider a rational response. I squeezed the customer's head like a grapefruit, pried open her mouth, and force-fed the dark granite paint sample down her oversized gullet.

I didn't do that.

"Fine, Fine," I said.

*

My lunch break couldn't have arrived sooner. I listened to Howard Hanson's Symphony Number Two, Romantic. I was occasionally distracted by the store's loudspeaker bleeding though my inferior headphones. I sat away from the others, in a corner, on a recliner. I sipped my cup of lukewarm herbal chamomile tea, laced with hazelnut-flavored, dairy-free coffee whitener. Several of the cashier girls were huddled at the end of a folding table; they were chatting with men from the lumber department, ignoring the TV as a news broadcaster drummed away about the plague of wars going on about the world.

The girls never talked to me, and I never talked to them. I always seemed to say exactly the wrong thing on those rare occasions when conversations did occur. Eventually, after years of rejection, I just stopped trying. I would even pull my hands behind my back and hook my thumbs when I passed them in the hall. Sporadically, they would say, "Hello," and I would say, "Hello." We would then go our separate ways without any encouragement to continue the exchange.

I sketched a loose collection of hills, cliffs, and a cove in a small pad. It wasn't a real place, just a worthless doodle. I broke the tip of my carbon pencil as my cell phone's vibration pulsed through my leg.

It was Colin. He wanted to share coffee and break cinnabuns in the University refectory.

"I'm already on my lunch, actually," I answered. He asked if I had sold the Norway and for how much.

"250," I said. "Standard's five. Keith Thompson asks for twelve." He knew I was unhappy about something. He had come to expect that. Soon enough, he was badgering me to join him that night at his regular public house.

"To Sergeant O'Keefe's?" I whined. "Seriously, I swear they lace their drinks with benzene."

Two of the girls overheard and looked my way. One of them chuckled. I ignored her.

*

I didn't want to be there.

Sergeant O'Keefe's Pub and Bar was barely either. It had changed hands three times and none of the new owners was Irish. They weren't interested in running a pub. The second added an unfulfilling strip club on the upper floor. That didn't go over well. The third owner replaced it with a pool hall and converted the lower floor into an eatery that mutated into a nightclub at 10:00 pm. The second or third owner dropped the second "f" from the name.

The volume of music forced everyone to shout at the top of his or her lungs. By the time I left the late shift and joined Colin, he had acquired two companions. To his left was a petite blonde with long curls and an exposed midriff. To his right was a modestly dressed wavy-haired brunette with perky cheeks, a sharp chin, and half-rim glasses. The girls were a recent acquisition. Colin gave the *"What can I say?"* expression with shrugged shoulders and open palms.

Colin Tavis couldn't be any more Scottish if he tattooed the Saltire on his arm, which he had. If God had put one more freckle on his nose, people would mistake it as cancer. Despite the heritage, he had no accent.

I was as average an Anglo-Saxon as nature could produce. Short black hair, round drooping cheeks, and deep eyes behind a dense brow to rival Scorsese. Not ugly in any sense but when the two of us went about town, Colin attracted bodies like an imploding sun.

"Girls," Colin shouted, "this is my best of best friends, William Weaver. Will, these are girls." They laughed.

I sat across from the three of them, a few inches closer to the brunette. That was intentional. Colin had already prepared his companions for my arrival, boasting about my attributes, my earnings, my potential for improvement in the years to come.

"I heard you paint?" the blonde asked.

Colin interjected loudly before I could unhinge my jaw. "More than paint, my boy here's a professional artist. Got stuff hangin' in museums."

"Really?" She snapped her head back to me.

"No," I answered frigidly.

"What kind of stuff do you paint?

"Landscapes." I could read she was expecting more. "Background landscapes for waiting rooms and lobbies."

"Like what?"

I offered a glance to the brunette, still quiet. This close, I noticed a beauty she was keeping hidden behind layers of clothes. I turned back to the blonde. "I do a pretty good rendition of the Eastern Carpathians..." I'd gone over her head. "They're mountains."

"Ohh--"

"Ever been to the lobby of the methadone clinic downtown?"

She looked at me vacantly.

"Why would I have been there?" she asked.

Colin's eyes dropped to his drink.

"Good point," I answered. I wanted to put a bullet through my head and claim an interpretation of Jackson Pollock across the dance floor behind me. "I-I have a rendering of those mountains there."

"Colin told me you sold a piece today?" she asked.

"Yes, I did, to the police station."

"Really. That's...unusual. Either way, it's something to be proud of."

"I guess," I answered. I knew I was coming off as someone sulking.

"Why do you say that?" she asked.

"It was crap," I grumbled. "I'm the artistic equivalent of a Swanson TV-dinner."

Colin shook his head.

"I like TV dinners," the blonde answered.

"Then I stand corrected. I'm a rice cake."

"That's only because you paint utterly forgetful paintings, William," Colin interjected. "Do something unique. Make your presence known."

The music shifted from a repetitiously annoying dance number to a hard rock song from the 80s. The change in tempo immediately caught the blonde's attention.

"Oh, I love this band!" she shouted then started clapping and undulating her waist around the chair.

"Who is it?" I asked.

This appeared an even harsher affront to her.

"Seriously?" she asked.

"No idea," I answered.

"AC/DC."

"Ah, right...of course."

Colin stood from his seat. He orbited the table and encouraged the blonde to join him in a dance.

"You a fan?" she asked as she stood.

"Not particularly," I answered.

The two of them parted for the dance floor. I turned to the increasingly attractive brunette staring blankly at me. Her black long coat was still buttoned and she clutched a vodka sunrise in her hands as if it was a self-defense baton.

"Hello," I began.

"Hi," she finished.

We said nothing else.

I figured she was as incongruous to the club scene as me, probably dragged as backup by an extroverted friend. She could have been a social worker or perhaps even an accountant.

After the third dance between Colin and the blonde, they finally returned. I stood from my seat as they sat. I caught a glance of a white silk blouse under the long coat of the brunette, probably tucked into pressed black trousers. She had also either come straight from work or had nothing else to wear other than formal clothes.

"Anyways," I started, "it's been nice meeting you both. I..." Colin was giving me a look, "need to work early tomorrow, so I'll bid you all good evening."

"Nice meeting you!" the blonde screamed over a remix of a Duran Duran song that didn't need to be remixed. The brunette offered a half-hearted wave, more like a half-second reveal of her palm.

Interpreting the vista outside the night club, I would use complimentary primaries to produce various shades of gray. I would make it gloomy and mysterious but avoid the drunks by the street, the errant garbage, and my Hyundai sporting a brand new scratch in the parking lot.

Colin had pushed through the crowd to intercept me outside.

"What's going on? What's wrong?" he asked loudly.

"I appreciate your effort but what solves your problems won't solve mine. This doesn't help."

"You just need to be sociable."

"But that insinuates I want to be sociable." I shook my head. "Last week, my Dad suggested I find a nice Asian girl. Seemed to think I would do better with someone with softer edges."

Colin nodded unconcernedly. "Did he almost say Oriental or did Asian come out right away?"

"He's not stuck in the 50s."

"He wants to be. Every time I see him, he reminisces about how great it was before 'the war'. The man's forty-five--what war?"

I couldn't help but laugh. I looked around the empty street. I made a step to my car as Colin resumed. "What's your problem? Is this about Aimee? She was a…" Colin trailed off, trying to find the appropriate word. "Moron. Most women would love that kind of crap."

It was a show of affection so old-fashioned as to be borderline melodramatic. I had known her for a few months through work. I offered a gift of a 500-piece puzzle. She loved them; I hated them. I spent ten hours putting it together. I flipped it over and wrote a message on the back. It was a riddle to lead her to a secret location in order to retrieve a more expensive gift—a book she had talked about wanting. In the fold of the book, I had placed a note expressing my desire for a date. She noticed the ink marks on the dull-brown backing of the puzzle pieces. Her head cocked to the side and she said the offer was sweet. She never finished the puzzle, never received the riddle, and never acquired the book. She quit and moved without telling me four weeks later. I found the book still in its hiding place two months after stashing it there.

"I'm just not playing anymore," I said. "I hate the game."

"The game?"

"The whole...you know the game--the game--the patterns of nonsense people follow when they try to impress the opposite sex. All the embarrassing and juvenile crap--the rejection. I just don't want to think about it."

"It was one setback. You can't lock yourself in your apartment and paint for the rest of your life."

"Never said I will...just for now I am." I held up my hands to stop another dispute. "Colin, I'm fine. I just don't like places like these, and I can't talk to anyone in them. Go back. Enjoy yourself. I'll see you tomorrow."

He didn't say anything. He just stared back.

"Go," I persisted, "the blonde's probably already picking a ring."

*

Rule one was indicated with an underline and was worth mentioning again. *No fakescapes.* It wasn't that important a rule. Since I couldn't use another artist's work as inspiration and sell it, it was a straightforward tenet to abide by. In this market, near-photo realistic depictions of actual locations sold far and above those derived solely from whim. Near-photo is stressed--buyers don't want photographs or they would buy photographs.

They prefer the slightly muddled and blurred memory only offered by a painting--that attribute of artwork to be lacking. It allowed the viewer to fill in personal qualities to make it perfect.

Rule two was connected to rule one--*use photos*. Nothing is worse that interpreting a memory. Might as well do something original. At the very least, I couldn't claim it as a real location. I owned a collection of three dozen personal favorites--high-resolution images found around the internet. I hadn't actually been to any of them.

Despite the selection, I often found myself replicating the same six images: Ceahlău Massif in Romania, Cliffs of Moher in Ireland, Hundred Islands in the Philippines, Iguazu Falls in Argentina (an unfortunate staple), Longsheng Rice Terraces of China, and Seven Sisters Waterfall in Norway. With the exception of Iguazu Falls, I made a point to find locations not offered by my competition.

Rule three was more of a suggestion, *No marks of Man,* but there were exceptions. The following buildings were allowed: Farmhouses, lighthouses, and windmills. The only vehicles allowed were farm equipment but they couldn't be in operation. Although competition often broke this rule, it did result in a reduced potential for sales. People were also not allowed and if an exception were to be made, the pigment of the skin couldn't be seen.

The fourth and last was obvious: *No Fantasy.* I know it sounds like the first rule, and it is worth repeating. However, this applies to the addition of mythology and the fruits of hackneyed fantasy writers. The last thing a hospital would buy is some fanciful daydream mocking the fragile faith of mourning families already in doubt.

*

Hanging clouds clung around green hills, pierced occasionally by jutting rocks resembling spear tips. Crescent shaped granite cliffs vanished into the distant fog to my right. The water at the base of the cliff bore the waves of an ocean and was more gray than blue. The tall grass around my feet was a luminous viridian, as if a painter had personally brushed each blade. Violet spear thistles danced around in an audible breeze. The tallest vegetation I could see was a family of junipers at the base of the closest hill, enclosed by a mob of ferns.

There were no marks of man was around me. I looked down the gentler slope beside the cliff and caught sight of a rock dwarfing anything else on the beach. It had no reason being there, too far from the cliff edge. Waist high and with a flat top, it waited for me to walk down and take it as a bench. With cliffs on both sides and the shadow of the rock spears behind me, the small cove was a secret refuge. It was a harbor meant only for me.

I slid and hopped over loose rocks, approaching the sitting stone. I noticed something on the rock...something black.

*

I opened the door to my father's house before he could answer. I had been given permission to call my father Robert, but I never did. "Dad?"

"In the basement!" came the shout through a thick Yorkshire accent.

Besides his rare trips down acid lane, my father wasn't all that eccentric. He only offered the façade so he could flirt innocuously with teenage girls at the local grocery store. He spent his early years building houses, living in them for a year, and then packing up and moving to another recent build. I had shuffled through a dozen houses before high school, all in the same city. We stopped when he developed Hepatitis B.

It wasn't a basement exactly, just the bottom level of the home our family eventually rooted itself in. It was a two-floor country house with slightly flattened A-frame. It was half-made of classic brick, the other half out of peach-painted wood. It had a front porch, a substantial second-floor terrace connected to the master bedroom, and a stone patio spreading from the rear door. A tiny loft was tucked under the roof.

He was rummaging through boxes scattered across the raw concrete of the storage room. It was next to the twin car garage, which was occupied by a '74 Volkswagen microbus and an '86 Porsche 911 resting on jacks.

"What are you doing?" I asked.

"Swimming trunks. One's I have upstairs don't fit." He had never taken a desk job. An aloha shirt was his uniform. He always sported a trimmed goatee and slightly frazzled hair always one inch short of being cut.

"I'm not hot on this trip you're taking dad."

"Actually, it's extremely hot in this trip. Yesterday was 40 degrees in East Timor."

"That's beyond the human tolerance for heat, you know?"

My father's head was still buried. "Wrong, that's 41. I'm solar powered, William. You know that."

"It's not the sun. It's the armed rebellion that worries me."

"Pfft...where don't we have wars on this planet? Seems like everywhere you look, someone's shootin' at someone else. Besides, you only live once. Got to do what you want to do." That was my Dad's motto, which he had repeated often. It started up after stomach cancer claimed my mother.

"Given the options, I'd rather you take a trip with *Lucy*."

"Acid only goes so far. I'd rather travel."

"Then go to Portugal or France. They don't kidnap tourists—"

"Bah," my father scoffed, "that's government propaganda." He finally emerged from the box and kicked it aside. Glasses were hanging off the edge of his nose. I couldn't remember him needing glasses, even at his age. "Besides, look at me. I'm worthless. The most expensive thing on me are my glasses." At that point, he threaded his finger through the glassless gap in the frame. I chuckled as my father dropped the glasses back into storage. He moved onto another box.

"Ahh, here they are," he finally said. He pulled out a pair of practically incandescent yellow swimming shorts.

"That's brighter than the sun," I said.

My father motioned me closer. "I got another in here, like this, only orange. Help me."

We began fishing through the remaining boxes together. "You sell the Norway," he asked.

"Yeah…250."

"Should have asked for five."

"It's a sale."

"So what's next?"

"Probably Eastern Carpathians--the Romanian piece."

"You've done that one five times. Do something new."

"Then it might not sell. Not really productive."

I removed the even brighter set of orange trunks. He clapped his hands and snatched them away.

"The secret of creating great art, son, is that you don't do it to be productive," he said. "The very definition of art forces it to be long, frustrating, and ultimately unrewarding in its process...and you never get your investment back. You always give more than what you receive, doesn't matter if its praise or money."

I began packing up the various scattered boxes and piled them back in the corner. "Thanks Dad. How long you going for?"

"Three weeks."

"You will avoid the rebels right? I mean, don't go looking for them 'cause I know you'll want to."

"Yes, yes, I'll keep to the beaches the whole time. I'm only there for a suntan and a swim."

"Good...cause I don't want to worry."

"Son, never worry. It doesn't matter what you do with your life, how productive you are. If you have children or don't. All that matters is enjoying your life, every moment, and screw anyone by telling you otherwise."

I watched my father take vacation after vacation, each in a slightly more dangerous location than the last. My mother curmudgeonly accompanied him until her death. The hostility of the environments he would visit only increased after. At first, it was slightly unhealthy regions like Mykonos and Recife. That migrated quickly to any beach not often touched by other tourists, scared away by tides, guns, or sharks. It was off to Capetown and Yucatan. Even that wasn't enough. His last few trips had him taking in the shores of Al Khobar in Saudi Arabia, Bali in Indonesia, and Khao Lak in Thailand.

My father also often repeated that when the possibility of death hangs over you every second, other methods of departure never held much gravity. My mother died when I was fifteen. My father trusted me to look after myself in his absence, which occurred more often as the years passed. He never ignored his son, and each time he planned his next excursion, he always offered to buy two tickets.

I never accepted.

*

I stared blankly at the cotton canvas. The television was off to my left. My computer sat idle to my right. I rubbed my wrists firmly, working up to each of my fingers. My photos were pinned around the outer edge of the workspace. I pulled the Carpathians off, gave it a look over, and then let it drop to the ash-gray carpet. The basement suite I lived in had only a small window, overlooking ten feet of concrete to the neighbor's house. Nothing hung from the walls, leaving the dark granite finish bare.

I snagged my other reliable selections, clumped them together, and dropped them on top of the Carpathians. I stared at the assortment of acrylic paints. Heavy bodied Raw Umber and Chromium Oxide, my lighter Ultramarine Violet and Pyrrole Orange. I stared at my soft gels, my flat mediums, and my set of Siberian blue squirrel brushes. The Paasche double action airbrush I rarely used. The mélange of dark tones marking up my beachwood palette. My painting knives were clean, the sponges rinsed.

I was trying to find that moment of clarity to encourage me to paint. I closed eyes and considered the random thoughts running through my head. My dad in East Timor. That brunette at the club. An incarcerated drunk gathering all his strength to lob spit from the jail cell to my painting on the wall. One thought surfaced, unwilling to be ignored. I opened my eyes slowly and began mixing.

I started with a gray-blue backdrop. I added hanging clouds clinging around green hills. Crescent shaped granite cliffs vanished into distant fog. The water at the base of the cliff bore the waves of an ocean and was more gray than blue. A luminous viridian.

Violet spear thistles.

A family of junipers.

The isolated cove and the waist-high sitting rock.

TWO

"Wow," Colin said.

I was still adding the final details.

I looked up from the canvas. "Really?" I asked.

Colin visited between classes. He was undecided in his major and had changed his mind at least three times. He excelled in every path but was unclear which one to settle with. His bike helmet was under one arm and a large black nylon backpack hung from his hand. "It's the best stuff you've ever done. So what is it? France?"

"No," I answered as I washed the viridian green from my brush.

"That view of the Moesa River in Switzerland you were talking about?"

"No."

Colin gave me a look. "There are 200 countries in the world. You gonna make me go through them all?"

"And you'd still be wrong," I replied with a smirk.

"No kidding, it's a fakescape?"

I shrugged, and then nodded. I wasn't positive it was.

"Not...sure?" Colin asked, bemused.

"Yeah...Yeah." I looked it over. It was exactly as I remembered it. The stone daggers punching through the clouds were out of view behind me. The cliffs reaching to the horizon were off the canvas to my right. "It's a fakescape."

"You're not just saying that. It's not the Shire and you're just messing with me."

"I had a dream a couple weeks ago."

"Of this?" Colin asked with a point. "Sure it's not a photo you've forgotten?"

I pointed to the pile of portraits by my computer. "Gone through them all."

Colin smacked me hard on the back. "Good on you...I'm impressed."

"I won't sell it." I wasn't being pessimistic. I knew my clientele. It might find a private buyer, perhaps through the website. But doctors, lawyers, car dealership owners, they all preferred something real. It didn't matter if they had never seen it. I could sell ten Grand Canyons a year if I wanted to.

"Don't be so negative." Colin leaned closer and reached out to touch something on the canvas but knew enough to stop an inch short. "What's this supposed to be?"

He was looking at the black mark on the rock. I bent down beside him. I couldn't remember putting it on. I had no memory of mixing primaries or breaking out the carbon black. The rock was shades of umber with dashes of ochre for accent. I couldn't get black from that. This was black. "I don't know," I said.

"Is it a mistake?"

"I don't think so." I did remember it being there in the dream.

Colin straightened himself. "I would add that to the portfolio." He pointed to the piece. "That, sir, is art."

I jokingly took offense, pointing at the others leaning against the wall. "What and these weren't?"

"Those are paintings." Colin nodded to the easel. "That is an expression of something you are trying to interpret."   "Didn't realize you thought so poorly of my work." I was goading. I knew he was joking.

"I didn't say that. Art is the intent of a creator to present something that can be interpreted by another. If there's nothing to unravel, it's an essay. Art's value is based entirely on the viewer. Art can also be a closed loop intended just for the artist. It's still art if the artist feels it is and shows it to no one. This confused you...It's art." He smiled and turned to leave. "I want Italian and you have a car."

I nodded and he left. I spent a few extra moments staring at the painting before I followed.

*

"Hmm...I think we'll take the Mansberg," One doctor said. The waiting room was shared between three of them, all general practitioners. They had matching secretaries handling paperwork behind them. The day was over and the last patient was quietly exiting. This was another low sale. I rarely got commissions. The police department never called back so I was hoping on moving the Longsheng Rice Terraces again. The doctors moved right over it.

I couldn't help but correct him. "It's Manhartsberg." They were looking at the prices, not the titles.

"What this one?" another asked while pointing at the fakescape.

"I guess it's untitled," I answered.

"What's it of?"

"Nothing in particular." I shouldn't have said that. I could lie and claim it was Holland.

"Is that a flaw?" the second had said, pushing his index finger against the black mark on the rock. I squirmed and fought the urge to protest.

"No...That's supposed to be there," I said.

"I'm not a fan of any of them," muttered the third between his teeth.

"We're supporting local artists. That was the point," whispered the first, audible enough to be heard by everyone in the room. He then spoke louder as if I couldn't hear the conversation. "We'll stick with the Mansberg."

I nodded and heard myself correct him. "Manhartsberg."

*

I got a couple feet closer to the beach this time. I saw around the cove, under the shadows of the cliff, what I couldn't see from up higher. My bare feet wiggled through the sand. The grains sparkled with an iridescent iron oxide. I had that color. The waves were harsh. The pull of the water would surely drag me from the cove. In the shadows of the cliffs, no one would ever see me. I was only a few feet from the rock. It was not a black mark but something resting upon it, like a coat or jacket.

I woke before I could see for certain.

I eventually got rid of the Longsheng Rice Terraces for $150 to a Chinese oncologist. The Manhartsberg from Austria went for two hundred after ten minutes of haggling with those three doctors, each of which made five times more money than me. This left the Hundred Islands and the new piece. I should have painted another Iguazu Falls. Those always sell.

I found myself dropping another canvas on the easel and mixing the gray-blue tones of the ocean backdrop. This time, I placed my view looking across to the crescent shaped cliffs, leaving the cove at the bottom left of the image. The sitting rock was still in view. The unseen dagger formations were sprouting off-scene to my right. This one only took me five days. My signature was visible on the bottom right as I mounted it.

I sold the Hundred Islands for $300, to be hung in the staff lunchroom of the local Wal-Mart. How I loved corporate directives. They thought the new pieces were too dreary. I still hadn't given either a name.

As I looked them over, I kept staring at the black mark. I thought if I removed it, the selling potential would improve. I shaded down some burnt sienna to give the illusion the black mark was only the murky edge of a shadow across the surface. As I dabbed the rock, I realized I had gone too dark. I glanced back at the pallet and saw the mix was close to carbon. I had no idea how I'd missed it. The black mark now "stood up" from the rock. It resembled a dark figure sitting upon the stone. The brush had perfectly created the silhouette of an individual on the rock in the cove. I almost pushed my head through the canvas. I wanted to reach out and pull the figure around. At the very least, I could ask them to move out of the painting. That was one of the rules.

I didn't own a doorbell and the entrance to the suite was at the back of the house. Colin banged on a nearby window to get my attention. I checked back to see if the figure was still sitting upon my rock. It was.

Colin's face looked awash in a morose misery. His jaw was sagging and his eyes had swelled. I couldn't read his expression, as I had never seen it before.

"What's wrong?" I asked.

Apparently, my cell phone had been turned off. He had been trying to call me since morning. He waited until he was inside before telling me.

*

Robert Weaver's trip was fulfilling. He received a leathery tan on a clothing-optional beach. He had photos of himself dancing alongside several local girls. He had dinner with a local celebrity—a boxer who drove a Lamborghini. He parasailed for the first time.

There was a photo of him smiling alongside a pair of good-natured rebel militia armed with AK-47s and RPGs. In one, he offered the "peace" symbol——the guerillas adorned in camouflage and grenades doing the same. He invited himself to accompany them back to camp where he taught their resident carpenter some advanced techniques to save time and timber. They allowed him to fire off a clip from one of their rifles. He peppered a tree, flaying off its bark. He concluded his day by sharing meat and wine over an open flame. They returned him to the road and offered him a chain necklace, which he wore proudly on the plane.

It was on the second connecting flight back when he suffered a massive coronary. He was gone before the plane landed. They figured it happened the moment the flight entered the local airspace.

The wake was a modest collection of friends and forgotten relatives, most from England. My mother was the religious one and when she passed, Robert rarely attended church. This would have been his first time in a year. I kept my emotions with conviction through the prayer services. At the funeral, we brought up the casket. I looked to my left and noticed Colin sobbing like an eight-year with a sprained ankle. We held each other and cried until encouraged by cousins I had never met to continue to our reserved aisles.

My father once joked he wanted his ashes flicked like a used cigarette from the window of his Porsche. Better still, he wanted them run through the car's engine system and fired out the exhaust. After the gag passed, he asked me to share a drink of his best port with his urn over a passing river and then accidentally drop it into the stream. I couldn't do any of that. The foreign relatives insisted he be buried, not burned, and placed above his wife in the family plot.

*

When I finally returned home, I notice the painting still waiting patiently on the easel. I took it down and stacked it with its brother. Colin wanted to take me out for dinner, something extremely expensive and horrifically unhealthy that he would pay for. He promised the restaurant would have high-back chairs and settings with multiple knives and forks.

I declined. After five days of banal banter with people I didn't care to know, I needed seclusion. Other than at the funeral, I showed little emotion to anyone, even Colin. It would have been nice to have known that brunette, to understand her, to have known her likes and fears. She could pull me into her lap and caress my hair as I cried. I lay on my mattress, descending slowly into the memory-foam. I stared at the stucco ceiling. I kept an image in my mind of my father with fluorescent shorts and a patterned shirt dancing on a beach with armed militia, never caring about how his life might end. He refused to be concerned about such trivial issues.

*

I saw the figure on the beach. As every other time, I was atop of cliff, overlooking the cove. The outline denied definition, blurry like muddled brushstrokes. It looked like a coat or long hair, running down a back. The waves were churning from growing winds from the north. I felt a pronounced chill in the air. A mist upon my face fell from heavy clouds encroaching overhead.

I approached slowly, the course sand drifting down the incline. The shape upon the rock was slender, almost emaciated. As I orbited the sitting stone, I found myself staring back at the stucco.

The next morning, before work, I received an email. It was a bankruptcy lawyer asking for a rendition of the Bohemian Forest. I had done it only once before. I ignored the message and opened the mixing jars of pre-made colors I had concocted the last time I attempted the dream.

I placed my view directly on the cove, closer to the sitting rock and drew the figure close to the foreground. I closed my eyes and tried to pull the image from the chaos of my subconscious.

I found her skin to be pale, not of death, just without the blush of makeup. The dark silhouette came from long, wavy hair. She revealed her high cheeks leading to a pointed chin. It felt correct. She faced away but turned her head slightly to offer a single eye to the painter. Her dark hair covered whatever she chose to dress with. She was still too distant to expose the color of her eyes.

"Where the hell did this come from?" Colin asked when I was finally prepared to display it.

"My dream," I answered, just sitting on the stool staring at her.

"That's inspired," he answered. He cocked his head and squinted at the particulars. She blocked most of the cove but the other paintings were resting against the floor around the easel. "Landscape is almost looking familiar."

"It would be nice if it was a real place," I replied. At least then, I could add a proper title and claim it as my best work. As a fakescape, other masters of acrylics, oils, and pixels created far better.

"Have you ever checked?" Colin asked. I gave him a muddled stare. "You ever noticed you painted same time of day?" He pointed to the second painting leaning against the fake leather couch. "When you painted the cliffs, you added the sun high in the afternoon." He then pointed to the first painting leaning against the wall. "When you did the rock on the beach, the light came from the right, which means you're facing north." He pointed to the newer piece. "Even the light on her face moves from right to left. You kept all of these consistent. Same time with the same place. Did you know you were doing that?"

"I don't think so."

"You have overcast clouds and an off blue ocean. Not only are you facing north, but you're also in the north." Colin crouched to stare at the painting of the cliffs. "Could be Norway or Scotland, Ireland even. Could even by Newfoundland or Nova Scotia. Perhaps you saw it in a book and didn't put it together. Better, perhaps it's an amalgam. Cliffs from Ireland, cove from Nova Scotia. I mean, if you look hard enough, I bet you find something close enough to claim as a title of this piece."

I knew he was wrong. I had searched for hours looking through my images, both retired and pending. I scoured my regular sites, the public domain images, the vacation spots of friends through facebook. Nothing had come close.

"Who is she?" Colin finally asked.

"No idea. I'm dreaming of it…and her, nearly every night. I've painted nothing else."

"How many of these have you painted?"

I sighed, removed the new piece from the easel, and placed it to lean against the ottoman. I walked over to the closet and slid the white plastic door open. I waded through my hanging pants and dress shirts. I removed the other paintings I had done of the cove. I rested one against the leg of the computer desk, another against the base of the easel, two leaning on the closet door, and a fifth beside the first against the couch with another resting above on the cushion.

Colin swallowed as he looked over the cove, the cliffs, and the sitting stone--different positions, different angles. Not a single one showed the whole of her face. She was always looking away, staring out over the water.

It had been three months and I had painted nothing else.

"Sold any of these?" he asked.

"Not yet." None of them had titles.

"I guess I should say good for you." Colin was obviously concerned. I could read it in his face and he wasn't even facing me. He walked into the kitchen and opened the fridge. The milk had expired. The butter was hard. The baking soda was saturated. The wash of various smells from dried fruit juices to sprouting vegetables lifted from the open door. The freezer was filled with frozen Salisbury steaks and no-name ice cream sandwiches. Colin closed the door quickly. "Why don't you come out tonight? No clubs, just dinner. Come on; let's get some sushi in you."

I entered the kitchen from the living room and saw Colin peeling an ice cream sandwich. "Not tonight," I said. "I want to finish this off."

"Wil, you need to get out," he said through a chew.

"I'm fine. Let's do tomorrow."

Colin squirmed as he took another bite. There was more ice than cream and I could hear him crunching crystals. He followed me back into the living room.

Colin navigated the maze of paintings. "Are you actually trying to sell these?" he asked.

"I assume I will...once I figure out why I'm painting them."

He stopped in front of the close-up. It was difficult to pull definition out of her face with a pale complexion against a backdrop of a cool gray sky. "She's attractive," Colin said. "Never knew you had it in you. Is this your dream girl?"

I sat on the stool and stared at her. It was the closest I had ever gotten. Every time I tried to walk around the stone, I was punished with opened eyes. A dog would bark outside. My alarm would sound. Heavy footfalls from the neighbor would thunder above.

"Always figured I was a redhead guy," I said, then shrugged. "Eh, what do I know?" Aimee was a redhead and terribly unhealthy. Jessica was no better. Painting was an adequate diversion from the aftershocks.

Jessica looked Asian but she was actually French and just squinted a lot. Aimee was an inch under six feet with most of that being her legs and neck. The dream shared none of their qualities. The dream's shoulders were despondent and her head wilted slightly to the side.

"She looks..." Colin started.

"Depressed," I finished.

Colin looked at the painting again, and then back to me. "You got that exactly right." His eyes fell off mine, to the closet behind me. He noticed the one painting I hadn't removed. "What's that one?

I spun around and noticed it sticking out from behind the door. "Must have forgotten it."

I had finished the fourth or fifth one. It was the only time where I decided to turn around and attempt to paint what was behind me instead of directly in front. I ignored the cove, the cliffs, and the expanding ocean. I brought out the greens and purples, painting rolling hills and flowers. Jagged mountains jutting from the magnetic fog. The mammoth stone spear tips rising from a shield of white clouds. I held it in hand and spun it around to display it.

"Just a realscape," Colin observed.

I scrunched my lips, puzzled. "What do you mean?"

He pointed to the piece. "Well...that's Scotland."

"What?" I asked, spinning it around quickly, checking for street signs or some unmistakable feature I had accidentally added.

"That's Scotland," Colin repeated.

"How do you?" I placed the painting on the easel, over the one already resting on it. "Colin, you've never actually been to Scotland."

"Google maps and Wikipedia. Trust me, that's Scotland. Why?"

"That's from my dream," I snapped.

"I thought the cove was in your dream."

"I turned around and drew the rest of it. I wanted to see if there was anything I was missing." I stood up quickly, snatching both paintings from the easel. I walked to the center of the room and positioned the other paintings to offer a complete vista from every direction. Colin and I stood in the center and slowly made our way around the painted landscape. "That's basically what I see at the start of every dream."

Colin nodded. "It's Scotland. That's only eighty thousand square kilometers. Could be anywhere? You ever see this before?"

"Never in my life."

"A travelogue? One of those Royal Scottish Tour books?" I shook my head. "Then maybe I showed you photos at some point—parents' vacation maybe."

"You're missing the obvious," I replied. He stopped and waited. I pointed to each piece as I pirouetted. "This landscape is complete. Every piece fits perfectly with another--cliffs to cove, to hills and stones. There is nothing surreal about this. And there is no way I could rebuild geography in all directions by seeing photos. I've stood here...maybe I'm supposed to."

"Supposed to?" Colin retorted. "Wil, what are you getting at."

I moved around each image and could feel myself ascending into the dream. I stopped and stared at the figure, the image I had put aside from the rest. I finally looked back to Colin. "Nothing," I said. "Nothing...don't worry about it. You know, I changed my mind. Let's get some sushi in me."

"Okay, Okay." Desperate to change topics. "My treat."

"I wouldn't expect anything less."

*

Booking time off was easier than expected, as I hadn't taken a vacation from the Depot since being hired. Every penny saved from every painting sold in the past year was thrown down for a coach flight. It would involve two jumps, a day stopover, and a midnight arrival in Glasgow. I had visited the local travel agency and milked them dry of every sightseeing and tour guide on Scotland. They tried to vend tickets to the castles Stirling, Urquhart, and Edinburgh. They offered the unmatched experience of setting foot in the Culloden Moor and Glencoe--two sites highly regarded for the numerous Scots massacred there. The guide sold tour packages promising full Scottish breakfasts, first class hotels, and a prestigious military tattoo. I ignored everything but kept the books.

I was told my father had left a nest egg and that paperwork would take several more weeks to process. I couldn't see my father being one to save coppers for a rainy day. No one stood up to claim inheritance because no one thought there'd be any. I was assured by the lawyer my name was the only one listed in the will.

I packaged a single duffel bag of two identical sets of trousers, three dress shirts, and numerous pairs of underwear. I purchased a GPS unit that doubled as a music and movie player. Within three weeks, I had everything planned out. I never asked myself why I was doing it. I thought to myself, *my dad wouldn't ask why. Got to do what you want to do.*

Some part of me wanted to tell Colin what I was planning but in the end, he was only afforded a brief answering machine message. "Colin, this is William. Just wanted to tell you, I'm leaving town for a few days. Going on a trip. My cell phone's on if you need to get hold of me. Be back soon."

Before I left for the taxi, I noticed my cell phone still on the kitchen table. I left it there.

THREE

I arrived late evening in Glasgow in early April. I agreed with Colin that the vista in my painting faced north. That could be a few kilometers from Inverness or up by Thurso. Knowing my luck, I'll have to hop a ferry to Orkney Island or even Faroe.

I rented a room for fifty a night at the Beersbridge Annex, a nuanced hotel five minutes from the center of town. It looked built from Lego where the builder ran out of red colored bricks half way. It was an appropriate comparison considering every other building I could see was awash in maroon. Green lawns across the street were enclosed by blue fencing.

The room was a showcase from the IKEA catalogue with faux-leather chairs with tables matching the fascia of the building, functional at the sacrifice of any aesthetic value. The bed was a double and stiff as wood. There was a plastic polish to the sheets and there was no toilet paper. I opened the drapes and looked into Firhill Stadium. It would have been advantageous if I liked football.

I couldn't pack my paintings so I scanned them into a portfolio of 8x10 matte sheets that I kept with the carry-on. The flight attendant, bus driver, and hotel clerk all asked where I was from, then followed that with suggestions of where to visit. Each one featured some great battle with the number of casualties equating the importance of the location.

"Call a taxi for you?" the clerk asked as I passed to leave. He had turned from a "she" in the span of dropping my luggage and changing my clothes. "Just missed the bus. It'll come 'round in twenty. Just outside, down Firhill and you can see the post."

I was in the right mind for a walk. The city center wasn't too far. I had the map in one hand and a folder of paintings in the other.

"Figured I might take it slow," I answered.

"Subway's only ten minutes. Town's farther than you might think."

"I have no toilet paper."

"I'll have some brought up." He was in his mid-thirties and his accent was barely discernable. "Was there a place in mind where you going?"

I opened the folder. "This will appear a little strange." I placed the pieces down on the counter, careful to keep it to landscapes and not people. "You know where this is?"

He riffled through them slowly at first, and then quickly got tired. "Scotland," he answered.

"Thank you," I answered sarcastically.

"Where you from?"

"Obviously not here."

"Been to the Culloden Moor?"

I folded the paintings back into the folder. "What is the fascination Scots have with their own kind dying?"

"Because we die better than anyone. There's no greater group of people walkin' this earth that leave it kickin' and screamin'. Every grave in this land is marked with the grooves of fingernails."

I shrugged. "Well, now I want to go there."

"Don't, it's a tourist trap. Castles are good, though."

"Any recommendations, one better than the others?"

"There's that one on the Loch Duich. Filmed Highlander there."

I looked at him cockeyed, "I didn't know that was significant. Let's start with lunch."

"Some eateries up the hill, walkin' north. Want to go somewhere interestin', you take the other direction, turn on Garscube. Not the most picturesque journey, but it gets better. Ride that to Cowcaddens. Bus'll go down Nile. You're lookin' for Buchanan."

"And what's there?"

"Mostly everythin'."

*

The old part of my home town consisted of night clubs with disco balls and lava lamps. Rooms were lined in colored patterned wallpaper. Glasgow's old town was older than my country, with churches made from granite budding off streets of cobblestone. The sky was overcast and the city was moist from recent rain. I stared through the condensation of the bus window. The city looked good this way. The shower had given the buildings a gloss. Back home, water would fall from plastic houses onto concrete roads. Here, rainfall lingered, mirroring the blue street lights and the red and yellow neon signs.

Even I couldn't render this justice. Buchanon was a walking street with old roads and new stores built under Victorian peaks. It was peculiar seeing a Starbucks and an Apple store built under church-like citadels, a mockery of progress. The city looked plucked from a medieval age granted you don't look down. That being said, I had dinner at Pizza Hut.

*

Lego walls probably would have kept the noise in better. The neighboring buildings and those around the block were student residences and the revelry bled through walls until dawn.

As it turned out a "full Scottish breakfast" involved haggis, neeps, and tatties. Two of those have potatoes, two of them have oats, and all three tasted better than expected. Each serving had the density of depleted uranium with the haggis a quantum singularity compressing oats, onions, and organs into a solid mass of nuclear protein. It kept with me most of the day.

I spent the morning at the People's Palace, early afternoon at the Hunterian Museum, and caught the last few hours of the Kelingrove Art Gallery. Each location superseded my expectations. Only the People's Palace was candid in its title. The Hunterian was a two-century-old chateau surrounded by leafy trees. The Kelingrove resembled a royal mansion hand-carved from orange clay and fired solid in place by a dragon's breath. It was there I cornered a pleasant little person named Conan Cormack. The receptionist claimed he was the local expert in landscapes. His accent was a stronger Highland English. The folder was open over a rail. We stood on the balcony overlooking the full-scale Supermarine Spitfire hanging a few feet from our reach.

"Well, the talent is budding," he began. "Lots of room for improvement. Disciplined hand. Good eye in contrast. Yours, I assume?"

"Yes, but-"

"It's a mark above the ones hanging in doctors' offices, I'll give you that." He flipped through the images, stopping at the rocky spear tips punching through the clinging mist around green hills. "Good strokes on the grass. Real effort with the blades-"

"I-I appreciate the criticism," I stuttered out, "but I was actually curious if you could recognize the location."

Conan was taken back. "Are you testing me?"

"Well, the photos were unlabelled and I was hoping on finding the real location so I can properly label it." The lie suddenly came to me and I realized it was golden.

"You're obviously a tourist. All this for confirmation?"

"More like an excuse. I was on my way."

He flipped through them again, and then returned to the dagger rocks. He kept on them long enough for me to speak up. "Look familiar?"

"Old Man of Storr," he answered decidedly. He closed the folder and slapped it lightly on my chest.

"Is it?" I asked. I had no idea to what he was referring.

"No, it's not."

"Excuse me?"

"Storr's bigger than this. Water's too close. But you are looking at Skye."

"The sky?"

"Skye," he corrected. "The island...of Skye"

"Are you positive?"

"Aye, nice place. Lots of painters depict it. Don't know where this formation is. Either way, good luck." He offered his hand and I accepted it.

"I guess it's off to Skye," I stated obviously, as Conan turned to leave. He spun back a few steps away.

"Good spot. Visit Donan castle. Filmed Highlander there, you know?"

"Yes, I got that."

*

The bus followed the A82 outside of Glasgow, through Stirling road in Dumbarton. It was one of the most beautiful drives I had ever been on, eclipsed quickly an hour later, outside of Loch Lomond. The hills and fields lapping the shores were swathed in a dazzling green I had yet to imitate. The bus passed through a dozen smaller hamlets, before finally departing from the water and cutting west towards Glencoe and Loch Leven. I could take a photo of every stunning scene. I could fill my folio with landscapes customers would drool over.

I awoke from a nap arriving in Fort William, the largest town in the region. I switched busses and my comfortable coach was downgraded to a twenty-seat bus outwardly carved from wood and driven by a kilt-wearing highlander with a glass eye.

We sped uncomfortably. I finally said goodbye to the relatively smooth road of the A82, which had been the path since leaving Glasgow. The bus rumbled over the uneven and broken tarmac of the A830. We were mere miles from the Atlantic when the road turned sharply north and pushed through to Mallaig. From there, the bus squeezed onto the Armadale ferry to cross the Sound of Sleat. I missed going to Eilean Donan Castle.

"Off to Skye, are ya?" the driver asked as the van snaked onto the A851.

"Yeah," I answered. I shifted to a closer seat. There were still a few unoccupied. "You stop at Portree?"

"Aye, I do." His accent was molasses. "Where you from?"

"Far away from here."

"Getting away from the problems of the world? Seems like new problems around every corner. This may be the last unspoiled patch of land on Earth in fifty years at this rate."

"What do you know about Storr?"

"What store?"

"Old Man of Storr."

He laughed pleasantly. "Pardon me. Aye, Storr. Just nort' of Portree. I've walked it even."

"Are there others like it? Sharp rocks like the Old Man?"

He jerked his head back to look at me. I could tell the other half-dozen passengers were concerned at my persisting distraction. "Are ya pullin' some'tin, lad?" he asked. "They're everywhere. What's it botherin' ya?"

"I'm trying to find a specific place."

"Well, you've come up wrong. Nothin' specific here. No one lives here wantin' anytin' certain. Even maps get them wrong. People still get lost in these parts. Good place to get lost in. What's waitin' for you then?"

"Probably nothing. I just need to see if it exists. I know it overlooks the ocean. There's a cove with cliffs."

The driver leaned over. I assumed he either had a good memory or was following the imperfections in the pavement.

"Lots of those here. Why the urgency?" he said. The driver carried an aura of sincerity about him. I paused, trying to gather a proper lie. "There's a girl involved," he said, not asked.

"How'd you know?"

"There's always a girl, lad."

I shook my head, feeling foolish. "Yes, there was," I heard myself say.

"What's her name?"

"I've no idea."

"None? She not tell ya', or ya' have yet to meet?" I looked out to the road he was ignoring. I wanted an errant sheep to wander or have the bus dangle a wheel or two off the tarmac to force his attention back to the road. He was even making slight adjustments to stay within the lines.

"That's conviction, lad," he continued. "You sure she's even there?"

I inhaled deep and blew out a big breath. The past month, I'd never thought of it. It was not as much of a desire to be here as it was a compulsion. I couldn't answer him.

"Well, I run drives to Storr," he said. "We could take it leisure-like, up the coast if it be suitin' ya?

I smiled. "I think I may do that, thanks."

The driver reached his arm out to me and offered his hand. I accepted and we held it a moment. "Nice to have met you, son," he said.

"Thanks. What's your name?"

"William," he answered.

"Mine too. William Weaver."

"Call me Billy, like all that know me. Weaver sounds like a local brand." He released his grasp and turned his head to verify he was still on the road. "You comin' to find your clan?"

"Unfortunately no. Mother was American. Dad was from London."

He smiled and turned his attention back to the road. "Oh well," he laughed, "nobody's perfect, ya' know?"

*

Portree was decorated by steep granite cliffs and hills of green cotton. Narrow roads were fringed by brick bulkheads descending into the lapping sea. The buildings were solid colored monopoly play pieces--blue, pink, yellow--placed flush against one another. As the bus rounded the tight corner of the road, I could see the rest of the town perched chaotically up the incline. Scattered black-roofed white houses peppered the knolls, eventually vanishing into a forest of spruce trees.

My destination was the Coolin View. It was nearly a century old but the sign advertising the free wireless internet tarnished the tradition. Like every other building in the center of town, the owners had elected a single gentle primary for their coat. With this one, it looked like orange-hinted yellow ochre. Forgetting my arrogance in convoluted color names, it was probably just a faded carrot.

I had reserved a single bed in view of the Sound of Raasay. Said view was a window half the size of my canvas. The sink was inches from my bed and inches from the shower, which occupied the same room as the bed. It was smaller and more expensive than the Annex but something about the atmosphere, the sociability of the hosts, made it welcome, comforting. Despite the size of the window, the expanse beyond it was breathtaking. Over the tops of trees and past the dozen boats drifting in the harbor, I spotted another line of colored houses jutting from the mainland into the sea.

I imagined breaking a few rules to render it.

Last night's sleep was more comfortable than I was expecting. I had opened my diminutive window and listened to the sounds of the sound to fall asleep. I was roused by the morning ferry.

Billy the bus driver had told me the day prior where to find him and when, two blocks down by Somerled Square.

"What you have there?" He said as I approached the bus, pointing at my portfolio under my arm. He was eating a sandwich behind the wheel, waiting for either the requisite number of people or for a certain scheduled time to depart.

"Paintings." His eyebrows perked. We exchanged a moment of silence before I realized what he wanted. I placed the folder on the steering wheel. He wiped the debris from his hands and opened the folio. He was immediately struck by the rendering of the cove, cliffs, and hills.

"Oh, you've been around," he answered candidly, carefully placing the work over to see another. "How long you've been in *Alba*?" I assumed that was Gaelic for Scotland.

"Only my third day."

The next piece was a closer view of the cliffs. Each image brought him closer to "her".

"But you've been before?" he asked.

"Uh...no...no. This is the location I'm trying to find."

"Now I'm starting to understand."

I wasn't sure what he implied by that.

"I'm sure it sounds crazy," I said as I moved through the other images, "but do any of these look familiar?"

"This land is rich, you know?"

"Very much, I know."

He stopped on an image of the dagger rocks and lifted it from the folio. "God had a bag of beauty and used it all here. There's so many hills and cliffs. You'll find it a hundred times over."

"I feel it's specific."

"Well, what did the photos, say?"

"Photos?"

"You didn't paint this blind, did you?"

I finally pulled out a lie. "No, no. The photos were unmarked."

He browsed the others, finally stopping at the figure. I looked down at the image and could swear her eye was more radiant than before I had painted it. A fluorescent but faded interior light twinkled off the highlights of her face.

"So this is her," he said.

"I kinda just painted her there," I admitted. "You'll have to excuse it." I reached out to accept the image but Billy rotated away to get a better look under better, natural light.

"Sad face, on a rock over the sea," he said. "Black hair and beauty. Like a sad fisherman's wife waiting for a husband never to return."

I leaned over Billy's shoulder to share his opinion. "I see-"

"Or a Selkie," he interrupted.

"Pardon?"

"Know well your mythology."

Myths, in my opinion, were just the faded spiritual tales of dead religions. It was the steps those legends took. They were canon, then they were superstitions, then bedtime stories. Sometime later, the last child stopped believing in them.

"Thought those were Irish?" I commented innocuously.

"Nooo, not at all. Well, I shouldn't be so hasty. In compromise, I'd say they were everyone's. Little bit Scot, Irish, little bit Faroe. Different stories, slightly the same and not."

"Well, I know-"

"But they're Scottish. Just how it is."

I tugged on the image to bring it closer. "Feels more likely this is just a despondent soul."

"Like she waits for something," Billy interjected.

"Perhaps...but I'm more concerned about the location, to be honest." That was a lie.

Billy finally released the image and allowed me to close up the portfolio. "Throw a dart," he said, "throw it again. Keep throwing, you'll run into a place like this eventually."

"That's discouraging." I placed the folio under my arm and sat on the nearest seat across and behind.

"You believe in God?" he asked.

"Not last I checked."

"Oh, what a shame. Else I would say leave it in his hands to guide your way. Without that, all you have is the dart."

There were only three of us on Billy's bus. He went on his tour like he was giving a speech without a microphone at a banquet. He shouted over the straining suspension and grinding gears. "Portree comes from King's Port when King James V visited in 1540. That's the official word, but why name a port you are landing in? Port's already there. Had a name already, I think. Probably older. We got stuff here dating before than Egyptians, you know?"

We had just passed the last house of Portree, north on the A855. The road was barely two-lanes and when the bus crossed an oncoming car, I was sure we would collide.

"You see there, Will?" Billy announced, pointing to his right. "That's Loch Fada. Any of that looking familiar?"

The road had drifted away from the Sound and the loch was the first body of water for thirty minutes. White telephone poles stuck from emerald hills on the left. The loch on the right was an unnatural blue, a bright ultramarine I had never thought possible in this world. I rarely used ultramarine, preferring Prussian blue for my water. The overall image would have been critiqued as amateurish if taken to canvas.

"No, not even close...but thanks for asking," I answered.

I looked ahead and could see the Storr, the jutting of rock in an ocean of grass. The Old Man was a spear-shaped stone sentinel standing next the Storr, looking over a wide stretch of water.

"This is where we stop," Billy announced upon reaching Loch Leathen. We disembarked and an athletic blonde with olive eyes and high cheeks took over. A tour guide. Billy remained with the bus.

"My name is Catherine. You can call me Cathy or Cat," she said. "We got a long walk so I hope you got good shoes." She lead us away.

A morning fog had yet to lift and the towering Old Man stood as a vanguard before a wall of grey mist. As we climbed, more of the loch opened itself before our eyes. By hour's end; we crested the first hill and the sun had finally driven the haze back to the water. I was still nowhere close to the Storr but could see nearly all the way to the Sound. Patches of moss were clinging to the peaks. Loose stones were scattered about the walking path.

And I knew this was not the place.

"Not it?" Billy asked as I returned to the bus after a thirty-minute hike.

"No. It's magnificent, though."

"You look dashed, son?"

"I'm not sure why I did this?"

"You got doubt?"

"No...just it's not Storr. Are there more that look like these?"

"Of course, if you go further north."

"Then I guess I go north." Even I could admit I was beginning to come off obsessed.

"This is far as I go today. After this, I go back and take another lot to Storr." He pointed to another bus. "That one goes north."

It was a cobalt blue Volkswagen microbus nearly identical to my dad's. This one was in shoddier shape with patches of rust, a missing logo, and wooden benches inside. "I'll keep a seat empty next time I come back up," Billy added, "case you change your mind."

I nodded in agreement and made for the microbus.

"Hey!" Billy called out to me. I turned around and caught a Zippo lighter aimed at my forehead. On it was inscribed "*Clíodhna*". I looked at the strange word and held the lighter back to Billy.

"Why this? I don't smoke and I never told you I did."

"It's always good to have the capacity to make fire."

I wasn't going to try to chew my way through the pronunciation. "What's this name mean?"

"Just the name of my mother. It's not a gift. I expect it back."

"Thanks for everything, Billy."

I thumbed the lighter and it ignited on the first attempt.

*

The other driver was not nearly as talkative as Billy and looked twice his age, and I didn't think that was possible. I also believed English was his second language. He greeted me with, "*Feasgar math.*"

I nodded and replied, "Afternoon." After which, he stuck with simple, slow words.

"We round Staffin to Duntulm castle." I paid the fee and kept quiet for the journey north. There was no one else on the bus. He drove frighteningly fast. The single-lane road only widened every few hundred feet, allowing the first car to arrive at one to yield to oncoming traffic. The bus driver never yielded and never slowed. The road eventually moved back to hug the sea and the occasional houses became more infrequent.

"Stop...STOP!" I screamed. The driver flinched and slammed the brake. I slid off the bench and fell on the rusted, rippled metal floor of the microbus.

"What, here?" he asked.

I propped myself back on the bench and opened the door. At first, I thought I'd seen hikers descending a hill until I realized the distance would have made them fifteen feet tall. The wayward sheep wandering around the base revealed their scale. I walked briskly to the hill crest.

"People are waiting!" the bus driver shouted. I ignored him as I fell under the shadow of the closest and tallest stone spear. They were rooted at the crown of a grassy knoll that tumbled into sheer cliffs off a torrent sea. The descent was steep.

This was it, or at least the closest I had ever seen possible. The rock formations were precise but I couldn't see the cove from this angle. The pigment of the sea and sky was the same as earlier by Storr, with a pronounced lack of gloomy gray. That concerned me.

I turned back upon hearing the horn honk. I ran back to the driver. He threw up his hands in disbelief. I shouted, nearly out of breath, "How long until the next bus?"

"Three hours, maybe, but the stop is two miles up the road."

I grabbed my portfolio from the floor of the bus. "It'll be fine," I replied and closed the door.

I heard the van sputter and lurch and grind second gear. A minute later and it disappeared around a bend.

The grass was wet and slippery as I scaled down past the rocks. The cliffs bent like a crescent, stretching into a thick mist westward. I approached the edge and caught myself short of the sheer fifty-foot drop to jagged rocks under a foot of violent water. The waves striking the crag were deafening. I followed the edge, occasionally glancing back up the hill to the spears. The noon sun was to my right, bouncing bands of light off shimmering blades of grass.

There was also no fog. Perhaps I had arrived too late. Perhaps the fog had passed and the sun was too high. The waves felt too violent.

Perhaps I was late in the day and the sun was setting--not rising—in the painting, meaning I'm on the wrong side of the island. I kept glancing back at the stone spears, waiting for that moment of validation, where every brush stroke and painted grass blade fell into place.

I didn't notice I had stumbled too close to the edge.

I fell under loose stones and plummeted along with them down the precipice. I flopped on my back, then my chest. I threw my feet down to anchor myself but only found my legs giving way, flipping myself in the air and fumbling down until I brought my hands up to protect my face. I heard a loud thud and my feet struck something hard.

As I pulled my sand-engraved hands from my face, I saw the solid chunk of rock that stopped my plunge into the sea. It was waist-high and set within a cove only a few feet from the beach. My left ankle had been bruised yellow and blue. I struggled myself up and sat upon the rock. Distant granite bulwarks outside of the cove broke up the waves before they could reach the shore. Here, it was quiet. The climb behind me was not impossible, but an effort given the injury.

My left hand wriggled its fingers through thick whiskers. I wrenched my head around quickly and saw the black leather hide resting beside me. I thought it was a coat. It wasn't. It had no buttons, shanks, or zippers. I picked it up and flopped the heavy hide on my lap. There were no tags. It was a pelt. It was not black, but grey with dark patches by the tail. There was no blood or hanging muscles, no bones. The whiskers about the face were still rooted in place.

I heard a splash.

I looked up.

She was staring back at me.

FOUR

And she was naked.

Dark hair flowed with a delightful whim to cover her curves. She had a foot in the water and stood petrified like she had always been there. I couldn't say anything. I was tense enough to cloud all reasonable thought. Her eyes moved to me and then to the pelt in my hand. I was still locked on her eyes. They were a luminous blue. Her cheeks were high and ran down to a sharp chin.

She was well beyond my reach but still close enough for me to admire every trivial detail. When I was forced into catechism, I was told a myth that the groove above our upper lip was from the finger of God, silencing a child after whispering the existence of heaven. She either was never told or was never forbidden to divulge it. There was only the slightest peppering of beige freckles about her face. Her dark hair converged to a widow's peak above a smooth forehead.

Seconds passed as coherent thinking was fighting to the surface of my mind. She was beyond any beauty that could be captured by my lukewarm painter's skill. The frigid breeze into the cove caused me to shiver but she remained, her skin looking as cherry-warm as the moment I saw her.

She was still glancing at the pelt in my hand. I realized I had yet to speak a single word. I finally lifted the pelt between us. She didn't respond. Neither swallowing nor trembling, none of the traits connected to anxiety. I swallowed. I trembled.

I could finally read vulnerability in her as if I was holding her soul in my hand. She was paralyzed with inaction, waiting for me to speak first.

"I'm-I'm-I'm sorry," I stuttered. My eyes darted between her and the coat. "I...uh..." I placed the skin where I left it on the stone and stepped away. "I'm sorry," I repeated. I made another step back. She shifted closer, like a stalking cat approaching prey, eyes locked on me. She pointed her chin towards the cliffs behind me and I heard a great crash of waves and wind against the rocks. The noise brought my attention away and when it returned, I saw the seal leap back into the water. She was gone.

"Oh no," I muttered. "No. No." I ran to the shore and sunk my runners into the wet sand. A swell rose up and soaked me to my knees. I saw the wake as her dark form paddled away.

"Wait no!" I shouted. "Please don't! Come back!" I could see the seal's head but she ignored me, gaining distance from the cove. "I never saw past this moment!"

She stopped. The seal turned her head slowly. Her eyes were still blue, radiant against her gray skin and the gray sky.

"I said I never saw past this moment," I repeated. The water was freezing and I began to shake as the sea claimed my body heat. My rational mind was begging me to step back but I couldn't. Every second I saw her was another moment where everything I had done and gone through was justified.

She proceeded to swim back to the shore, flopping onto the beach some distance away. I followed her back onto dry land, my drenched trouser legs still sapping my ability to stand without shaking. I approached the sitting stone but only placed my hand upon it.

"You were on this rock." I pointed at her. "And you left that there." The seal waddled closer to the stone and lifted her front flippers to prop her front half onto the stone. She lifted her snout and chirped a high-pitched whine. I heard another wave crash behind me but I was more prepared and I didn't turn my head. She called again and I heard another bellow, even louder. I realized what was happening and I took the risk she would still be there. I turned back to the cliffs and when I returned to the seal, the pelt was resting back on the rock and she was concealed behind the sitting stone.

"Oh my," I managed to mutter. I unbuttoned my heavy wool and polyester black longcoat, removed it, and placed it over her pelt. "Take it...I took yours so it's only fair."

She reached her hand slowly and pulled the jacket over to cover her back. Her hair was still sticking to her skin.

"My name is William," I started. "William." She stared back, looking up through her brow. "Family's name is Weaver. I'm William Weaver." I had no idea on the scale of an idiot I was appearing to her.

"Dè 's cùis..." She whispered. It was soft and barely audible over the waves. It was a stutter. I could tell. I leaned closer. She spoke carefully and slowly. *"Dè 's cùis leis gu bheil thu an seo?"*

I knew she understood my lack of comprehension. "Pardon?" I murmured back. She pushed herself higher on the rock. I knew the jacket wasn't done up but I couldn't break from her eyes.

"*Cò às a tha thu?*" I assumed she was asking by the inflection in her voice. Only the sitting stone stood between us.

"I have no idea what you're saying," I muttered through a smile. She cracked a smirk back.

"*Chan eil thu às an àite seo.*" I would have sold my soul to the nearest devil to understand her. It was important enough for her to return to shore to tell me. I wanted to know how she was here, where she was from. Did she belong here or was she drawn as I was? For all I knew--for all I hoped--she was thinking, and perhaps saying, the same thing.

"You are exactly as I imagined," I said.

"*Dè a' chànain a th'agad?*" she asked.

"English," I answered. She smiled broadly and a dimple sunk in her right cheek. "Wait, what?"

"*Cum ort ag ràdh,*" she said louder, inching closer. I remained where I was, shocked at her question and her encouragement. "*Cum ort ag ràdh,*" she repeated

I had no idea how this was happening. "What should I say?"

"*Tòisich le ainm d' athar.*"

"All right. My father was..." Logic took hold and I shook my head. "Wait, how can I understand you?"

"*Chan eil cànain againn.*" She paused. "We learn our words from others."

Describing her voice as celestial would be incorrect. I could see her voice carrying a song to enchant ship crews to wreck. Her accent wasn't

Irish. It wasn't Scottish. I honestly didn't know what it was. Granted I wasn't an expert on regional dialects.

"So are you speaking my tongue or am I just understanding yours," I asked.

"I have never asked that," she answered.

I placed my hand on my chest. "William Weaver."

"Skye."

"Like this island."

"That was thoughtful."

I laughed back.

She tilted her head, confused but buoyant. "Would you prefer another?" she asked.

"Another?"

"I could call myself *Sgiathach. Muirenn or Cailleach*, if you would...If you would prefer." I noticed the stutter and wondered if she was nervous? "As I speak now, it is Skye."

"Very well," I answered. A moment passed slightly beyond uncomfortable. I had difficulty staring into her eyes. I would often drift to her nose or her chin. She was nearly a statue. I felt I should say something poetic or poignant to mark the moment. "Uh..." was all that emerged. I was a painter, not a writer. If I were any more pathetic, I would ask her if she had seen the latest football match. Perhaps I would comment on the status of the weather and remark about how gray the water was. I counted the silent seconds passing. I expected her to offer some excuse about having plans, fish to catch, and dart off without hesitation. Say. Something. You idiot. "Uhh..." I uttered from a gaping jaw.

Bravo, be sure to include this in the great fable of The *Selkie and the Pathetic Tourist.*

"I am not sure what happens next," she said.

"Neither I," I answered. I smacked my dry lips. "I apologize." I paused a moment. "For-For the coat. Taking yours. I-I didn't intend to take it. I...didn't...know."

"Accepted," she whispered. She caressed the lining of my jacket. "Thank you."

"You're welcome." Nothing new was coming to mind. I knew a weather comment was about to surface. "I...I'm not sure what to say...I'm somewhat dumbstruck."

"Likewise," she whispered. I hadn't considered that.

"You're the one that just crawled from a sealskin."

"As normal to me as clothes to you. More so."

I finally gathered the courage to ask. "How are you here? Why—"

She held up a finger quickly and her smile turned to a reserved grin. "Do not ask why? Do not give in to questions. That is how we went away."

"Okay. But the dream." I finally leaned in an inch. "Did you have it as well? To be here at this time?"

I was trying to avoid looking at her figure as she lifted herself to rest on the stone. It was unavoidable but the folds of my jacket took delight in denying me any details. Traitor.

"This is my place," she answered. "I chose it because no other eyes have seen it. I am given one day to take to land." There was space on the rock for me to share it with her but I didn't dare be so presumptuous. That was the rational answer but truthfully, it hadn't occurred to me yet. "And

you are here on that one day," she continued. "Where are you from? A
clan."

"No clans where I'm from. A city in a country across an ocean. All
with names that I've truthfully forgotten at the moment."

"And who do you serve? What kind of ruler. A king?"

"No kings where I'm from. Even our gods are fading." My heart was
slowing. I could feel myself calming. Her manner was disarming. Even
the cold of my soaked legs had started to feel warm. The waves behind
me had fallen to a hush. My senses were coming back. She was sitting on
her coat, wearing mine, with nothing underneath. She had come from the
sea hidden in the skin of an animal and never once did I doubt it.

"We follow only three things," I continued, "our dreams, our currency,
or others strong in the first two."

"And which did you choose?"

"I'm here, am I not? It was a foolish and childish thing. And you, I
imagine, follow nothing but the current."

"And the impulses my heart commands."

I looked behind the rock and grabbed the portfolio, which I had
understandably forgotten about since I fell down the cove. I slinked my
way to the stone and sat beside her. I opened the folio and showed her the
first image, of the cliffs, cove, and sitting stone.

"I followed this," I said. I offered it to her and she held it like it was
still wet with paint. She immediately noticed the second image underneath
it, of the cliffs bending like a crescent into fog.

"Did you create this?" she asked.

"It's all I was ever good at. Not even sure about that either. I've
thought of nothing else for the past four months." I offered her the second

image, then the third, of just the cove and the stone. She accepted each one, the fourth showing the spear-shaped rocks up the hill, the fifth showing her silhouette upon the stock. "And this," I added as I showed her the final image, of her looking disheartened to the sea.

She caressed her hand over the image, keeping her fingers just off the surface. "I rarely get the chance to see this face," she said.

"I didn't do it justice."

She looked over the image, taking notice of the color choices, the flaws of an undisciplined hand. I wasn't sure she knew it was a copy. She moved her attention to the other pieces. "They are beautiful." She lingered on the first one, and I felt a sadness as her jittery fingers ran along the edge, as if the image reminded her of an old pain.

"They're yours," I said.

She firmed her lips and smiled. "Then place them safe so they don't spoil." I opened the portfolio and allowed her to slip in the paintings. As she did so, her fingers rolled over mine. "You are cold," she said.

"Far from it," I replied, and in truth, her touch brought color back to my face. My digits were still trembling.

"But you are shivering?"

"I'll be fine."

"You should find shelter."

"I don't want to leave this spot," I answered carefully.

Skye stood up and buttoned the coat. I could see below her knees, at her rosy, thin legs leading to untrimmed toenails. Beads of freezing seawater clung to her shins. "I have no reason to depart. I'll help you find driftwood."

I stood beside her. "I thought you would be bound to the cove?" She didn't answer, only offering another smile as she walked along the beach. The incline under the crag was considerable and her feet stumbled across the loose stones.

I caught her as she shifted her balance.

"Sorry...first steps after many years," Skye said. I offered her my hand. I wasn't sure how she would react. She took it promptly.

"Happily accepted," she said.

*

Finding wood along the edge of the cliffs was easy. Finding a dry spot behind the sitting stone was easier. All the while, I was rolling the thought over in my mind about the ignition source. Of all the times to have a lighter and never needing to smoke. I guess Billy the bus driver was right. It's always good to have the capacity to make fire. I grabbed a tissue from my pocket. I gathered up some twigs. The Zippo lit on the first attempt. Although it spewed a lot of smoke, the dried driftwood eventually took a flame. I noticed that Skye didn't react to the lighter. I figured she was either smart enough to know man would still build and innovate or she had been checking up on us from time to time. It would have been difficult to avoid with cruise ships, fishermen, and all manners of war passing overhead.

"Robert Weaver," I finally answered as I fanned the fire. I looked across to see her radiant eyes through the rising embers. I felt a lump in my throat as I repeated it. "...My father was Robert Weaver."

"You are saddened by his name."

I sat down some feet away, her at the south of the fire, me at the east. "He died some months back," I said.

"And a mother?" she said, her voice still soft, almost whispering, though I could hear her as clearly as if she was speaking directly in my ear.

"Years before," I answered. "Just me now, no brothers or sisters. Cousins I don't care to know. And you? I can't help but ask questions, it's my nature." I held out my hands to warm them. She kept herself bundled in my jacket. I was sure I would never wash it again.

"I understand. Best to avoid the why. Never ask why. I know that is the greatest question and the one your people cherish the most, but it is the one I am incapable of answering." I nodded. I didn't fully understand but I knew then that my not understanding was the reason why I couldn't ask.

"It's my nature," she continued. *Where* is easy. *Who* easier. *When* is a little tricky. *How* and *why* are the difficult ones. Asking and the answering that followed is why you do not see the likes of us anymore."

"Us? And how many..." I couldn't help but be curious. I wondered if the answers she needed to avoid were the ones that explained how she was here, or how I was here. Did she not want to know, or did she truly not know. If she didn't, was there a reason at all. "Sorry...do you have a family?"

"Never took a husband," she answered. I almost blushed. "Animal or man." Then I blushed. "I have not seen the likes of siblings in many years. We each have our rules and realms. They grow smaller each year."

"As our world grows, yours vanishes." I assumed.

"It is not so much your world as your questions. You wonder why rocks fall. Why birds fly. Why boats float. So you answered those questions…and soon we could no longer fly or float."

"Then I'll never ask why you came," I said, "as I truly don't need to know." She smiled, which brought out the dimple, and then she nodded. "Have you been at the sea long?" I asked. "Do you visit land often?

"No," she said, "we each have rules we must follow. They make no sense and there is no reason for them, yet they are undying. For me, I can only take a day on land every ten years. By the end of that day, I must decide to remain human or return to the sea."

I looked up at the sun, well past the afternoon, and then checked my watch to verify the time. It was two minutes past three.

"So when does this time end?" I asked.

"Do not worry about that."

"Then I won't."

"And your world?" I noticed she had rolled an inch closer to me and was leaning slightly to avoid looking at me through the growing flame.

"What would you like to know?"

"The last time I discussed human matters, your news was screamed from men standing on boxes, and it was often months late from current affairs."

"We've cut that to seconds. What news did you hear last time you listened?"

"That a man had frozen moments of time on paper."

I drew in a big breath and let it all out quickly. I couldn't remember when the first photograph was taken.

"That's a lot to catch up on."

Skye told me she hadn't intended to avoid the many marks of man across the world. However, in her swimming circles, she never saw much of technology. She saw the rapid progress of fishing, from nets thrown off canoes to immense synthetic lattices kilometers long strung between goliath trawlers. She watched a submarine drift by her quietly nearly fifty years ago and then saw another twenty years later that looked the same. Noisy cruise ships would navigate through the lochs and sounds of northern waters. She would playfully flop around the surface, smacking a fin on the water. She always avoided photographs, ducking under before the flash would spark.

I told her about the fall of monarchs, about the rise of republics, and the wars which came about because of these events. I told her how we took to the heavens, claimed the moon with a footprint, and connected nearly every human soul though a nearly imperceptible network of lights.

Never once did I feel I had lost her. I knew what I told her distressed her somewhat. I initially thought it was because of mankind's fall from faith--which most of us no longer believed in the unreal. If we did, it was only out of tradition and repetition and not true faith. I told her many people still believed in God or gods.

I realized that was not it. To her, faith was another form of explanation. Before science began making sense of it all, gods were being invented to do the same. I didn't fully understand it yet, but I knew pushing more answers would result in an explanation, which was always the problem.

"I wish I had taken to land sooner," she said with her requisite beaming expression. It was then I realized she had moved to within reach. I looked at the fire and the sea and noticed I had moved as well, meeting her in the middle. Her toes were brushing mine. My socks and shoes had dried hours earlier and were resting on the rock.

"I think my wish well is dried up," I answered. "After this day, I can't wish for anything else for the remainder of my life. We wish for the impossible. We hope for the achievable. We expect the realistic. How can I desire anything more?"

Her smile faded somewhat and her eyebrows sunk. "Will you demand it of me?" she asked.

"What do you mean?" I didn't know much of Scottish mythology but knew enough about the various legends dealing with faerie women and the conditions to win their affection. I had no idea how much of that applied here.

"Will you take my power and command me as you will?"

I couldn't imagine such a question being asked. The stories all recounted fishermen, traveling merchants, and soldiers, using trickery to secure the hand of a fairy. It involved deception and near exploitation. I would have no part of it, despite knowing it may doom the dream.

"I would never force you to do anything."

She reached her fingers to caress my exposed forearm. My hairs stood at attention. "And what if I wish you to," she whispered.

"I can't," I murmured. "It's not right."

I had no idea if I could apply any human qualities to her. If she was the seal and spoke to me, regardless of her language, how foreign would her mind be? How could we share a single common interest? Would she be driven by pure instinct? Would she rate me on the size of my neck, my capacity to lift great weights? The few myths I did remember, the faeries in them were always depicted as vain and superficial. They were only drawn to the iconic images of male perfection.

She kept quiet for a moment as I tried to understand a mind that could be as alien to me as a dolphin is to a dog. Even with a common tongue, would we have any hope of understanding each other? Was she humoring me, testing me? I was never a confident aggressor even when the objectives were human. Women were confusing enough. Skye was probably a thousand years old. As another minute passed without her saying anything, I grew more worried.

"I understand and I am sorry," she finally said. I instantly assumed the worst. "You do this out of respect and I placed you in a position to force you from character."

"Nothing to apologize. I simply don't know which answer would suit you, which answer you would prefer. Not knowing, I defaulted to honesty."

Her fingers rolled across my forearm until they met and wiggled into my hand. "That would have been the correct choice."

*

There were no more uncomfortable moments, no embarrassing pauses or misspoken phrases. The sun had fallen upon the rock spears and sacrificed its lingering light to the waning moon. Two hours later and the cloudless sky was speckled in a mélange of stars and satellites. She was resting her head on my chest as we leaned against the sitting stone, inches from the edge of the shore.

"These hours are not enough," she said. "Not to satisfy and not enough to resolve." I hadn't checked my watch in hours but I knew we only had a few minutes left.

"You'll go back," I stated. "I know that."

"You are right to an extent. I am bound to this land, as long as I remain of the sea. I could make a life," she then looked up to me, "but you are not from here."

"That could change."

"That is too much to ask."

"Ask?" I answered. I brought her up and held her shoulders. "How could I not? Looking back, I'm not sure why I did it. I don't know really why I came. I never got lost. I always asked the right people at the right time. I never took a wrong turn or was lied to. Every thought and event brought me here to this point. I did all this willingly and I won't let it pass as a fading memory. This could never happen, but it did."

"Don't ask why."

"I won't...you and I just happened, without cause. There was no reason, was there? The moment we ask why is the moment we must acknowledge it could never happen. If we ask how is when it stops ever happening."

Her eyes swelled as if to shed a tear, but she didn't. "I think you finally understand."

"Then don't ask me why I would stay here."

"I may not know much about your people except that to make a home here would take time. You are a visitor. You must own land and raise walls. I have only a few moments before I must take to the sea."

"You said ten years, correct? Ten years before you can return to land?" She nodded. "Will you be here?"

"You would do this?" she asked, then smiled. "Here am I asking." She stared through my eyes into my soul. I could see into hers and felt that under her skin and behind her eyes was not a collection of nerves and muscles but a consciousness unbound by instincts and primal urges. In the same way, I was bound by genetics and an evolutionary heritage, she was compelled by chaotic and unexplained rules she could never question. She would be the patient one and she knew what I was offering. "Yes," she answered. "Ten years, I will return, to the day, on the second I can set foot."

"Consider it a promise held."

She rolled on her knees and leaned into me. I could see down my jacket but didn't do so. Her lips were moist and salty. Her tongue moved as water around mine. The kiss felt like a lifetime. I could taste the ocean. She pulled away and stood up. "You are such a man, William Weaver."

She turned from me and retrieved her proper coat from the sitting stone. She looked back and saw me covering my eyes. I knew she didn't care and I cracked my fingers open as she dropped my jacket.

I won't describe what I saw as she went into the sea.

It was meant only for me.

FIVE

It must be stated that at no point was I ever rocking back and forth on a kitchen chair, muttering to myself incoherently. I never sat in a recliner, in my underwear, eating *baconaise* from the jar, staring at my paintings. I wasn't a shut-in. I didn't quit my job…at least not right away.

I woke up beside the rock just after dawn. I was cold. My ankle still hurt, and I had a slight headache. My coat had fallen onto the beach. The portfolio sat behind the stone. I looked out across the sea and wondered if she was staring back. Even if she wasn't, she was still close by. This was her sea.

I crawled up the hill and met my stalwart centurions, the dagger-rocks I was sure to assign names to later. I limped leisurely back south. A vehicle never passed me. I eventually made it all the way back to the Storr by the afternoon.

Billy the bus driver was already sitting on the bottom step of his empty bus. He read a local paper.

"Got room for one more?" I asked.

He looked and lit up. "How's my namesake, lad?

I held out his lighter. I flicked the cover and lit it with a passing thumb. I closed it and handed it back. "You have no idea how useful that was," I said.

He accepted and pocketed it. "Well, glad I could be of help. You look cold and soiled. You slept outside." Billy looked past me, down the road, and then around the parking lot. "What bus? Will, my boy, you weren't stuck here the night, were you?"

"I found it, Billy," I answered.

His brow perked. "Did you now? And was she there?"

"Something tells me if I said no, you wouldn't believe me."

"Aye, right on that. So what happened?"

I stepped past him and boarded his bus. "I'm smiling, aren't I?"

*

"$475,250," the lawyer said.

I was obviously taken back. I leaned in. He was behind a desk of black glass in a room of fake wood and real stone.

"I'm sorry," I coughed, "could you repeat that again?"

"Four hundred and seventy-five thousand, two hundred and fifty," he said slower.

I was sitting alone in a very big chair. I was not a small man but I looked like a child in it. "How the hell did my dad manage that?"

"Wise investing."

"Is there anyone contesting?"

"No, quick and painless," the lawyer answered as he splayed the folder in front of me, revealing the dozens of documents I needed to sign. "You're nineteen, correct?

"Yes."

"So you're entitled to it all now."

"All of it?" I asked, still acting indifferent.

"After cuts for government and myself. May I suggest a financial planner, invest most of it wisely, pay out the rest weekly like a paycheck. Still gives you the option for say, a car or a house."

"A house," I spoke up.

"Yes, if you wanted to buy a house."

"Or build a house."

"Yes, of course."

*

James placed a collection of tekimaki and nigiri between Colin and myself. He was the owner of the local sushi bar and the best of its kind anywhere in North America. Despite being the grounded and successful son in a proud Korean family, he was the dreamer among his kin.

Colin was obviously concerned. I was looking through a large digest detailing foreign land purchases.

"Thanks, James," Colin said.

James pointed at the pieces. "Kamikaze, spicy salmon, and caterpillar roll. The red tuna is especially good today."

I snagged the avocado draped reverse roll filled with tobiko, tuna, and cucumber. James took the empty seat next to us.

"So what you guys talking about?" he asked. He was still wearing his white chef's hat and coat embroidered with the red words *Iron Chef*.

Colin crammed a crunchy kamikaze into his mouth. "He's loaded," he said through chewing.

James's eyes lit up and he turned to me. "You sold a painting? How much?"

"No," I answered, reaching for a maguro.

"Turns out his dad had a fortune," Colin interjected.

James looked at the book I was skimming. "And you're looking at property?" he asked. "Good investment."

"Yeah, empty plots actually," I said.

"Like printing your own…" Colin said but trailed off. His attention focused on the title of the book. "…William?"

"Hmm?" I looked up and asked.

"Why Scotland?"

"Scotland's a nice place," James volunteered.

"William," Colin said, "Why…Scotland?"

"I liked it," I answered, burying my head back in the book.

"You were there a week."

"You meet a girl?" James asked.

"Kinda, yeah," I answered.

"Kinda?" Colin asked. "You don't *kinda* meet a girl and then buy land in Scotland."

"Dad's probably a realtor," James joked.

"Here it is!" I shouted and gathered the attention of everyone else in the lunch service. I concentrated on the entry.

"What?" James asked.

"That's almost perfect. Plus 57 degrees, 32 minutes, and 25 seconds by negative 6 degrees, 8 minutes and 32 seconds." I threw down the open book and pointed at the plot. "That's IT."

"You were looking for some place specific?" James asked.

"Not the painting," Colin said. It felt more like an order.

"Yeah," I answered unapologetically.

"Are you insane?" Colin snapped. "Did it *kinda* look like it or was it close enough that you filled in the gaps?"

I stared at him. "Colin, it was perfect."

"Show me a picture."

"What?"

"Show me a picture," he repeated.

"Didn't take one."

"Seriously?" Colin retorted. "Okay, the girl. Let's see her." I could tell he was getting angry.

"The girl?" I asked.

"Yes, the girl."

I paused, realizing how he was going to react. Part of me didn't care. "Don't have one."

Colin fell back on his chair. "Of all the…" He firmed his lips and went over the thoughts in his head. "William, I love you and all, but this is going a little far. It was weird enough when you were painting all of those. Now I'm thinking you're doing it to get away from what happened."

James started rolling his head back and forth between us like a tennis spectator.

"I'm not running," I said.

"You're buying a…" Colin pulled the digest closer to him to read the entry. Even though upside-down, the price was easily legible. "A hundred-thousand dollar plot of land in Scotland after being there for week because you *might* have met a girl that matched a painting you made. Come on?"

"Don't diss the guy, Colin," James interjected. "It's like you're saying it wasn't real."

"The odds are astronomical." Colin was escalating. He was all logic. I would learn later the proper term was *noegic*. "You'd get hit with Soviet satellite before something like this could occur."

"Stranger things can happen--" James said.

"No it can't," Colin interrupted, "people just say that. Besides, you're catholic."

"That shouldn't mean anything," James answered. "Neither is Will. You're being awfully argumentative."

Colin took a moment to breathe and grabbed a maki. "Don't you have Sushi to roll?" he asked.

"Nah, I'm good."

"Why can't you support it?" I asked Colin.

"Look at the signs. Your dad died. World's going to hell around us. People go through strange emotional periods when stuff like that happens." Colin took a moment, closed his eyes, and calmed his tone. "I'm worried, dude…seriously. I mean, I didn't want to say anything when I saw all those paintings. But dropping everything and going to Scotland, for what? You think if you stay there, she'll magically show up?"

"Colin," I answered, "you have no idea."

"I thought you'd support it," James said.

"Even I'm smart enough not buy a plot of overpriced land outside of a power grid," Colin snapped, losing his temper again. "Jesus, William, you'll spend every dime on this. For what? You can buy land here. Actually, make you money."

"Here am I thinking you'd understand," I muttered. How disappointing, but I knew his reaction would be pessimistic. I stood up and removed my wallet.

"Sit down," Colin pleaded. I removed fifteen bucks to cover the meal and tip and handed it to James. He accepted.

"No," I pushed between a tight jaw, "think I'm done."

"You're being such a little child," Colin snapped. "Why are you doing this?"

I froze, the open wallet still in my hand. "What?" I whispered.

"Why are you doing this?" he repeated louder.

I smiled and coughed a little laugh. "I don't know." I turned around and took my time to the exit.

James and Colin watched me leave.

"I think it's a great idea," James heartened.

"Go cut fish!" Colin snapped.

*

He was right about one thing. There was no power on that plot of land. Nothing. Great view was all it had going. Cliffs were too steep. Waves were too dangerous. The cove was too small for any decent sized boat and the rock and coral bulwarks out from the shore would tear passing vessels to shreds. It was in the middle of nowhere. Not one moment passed where I wasn't thinking of solutions.

I wouldn't be running a boiler in the furnace or cooking from a Dutch oven in the kitchen. I wondered if adding electricity would break some rule. I had no idea how her world worked. No one knew, not even them. At least, that was the impression I got. Therefore, it shouldn't matter what I built and how I built it.

It would have power. Specifically, a 10Kw whisper-wind off-grid, variable pitch wind turbine. I read Scotland supported the use of wind power and the location looked perfect. Solar was out of the question given the number of clouds. That would eat up forty thousand counting pole and installation. I borrowed the plans for my dad's last house. A two-floor country house with a slightly flattened A-frame. Half classic brick, half peach-painted wood. A stone patio from the rear door. A tiny loft under the roof. A front porch. A second-floor terrace connected to the master bedroom.

I gathered my father's building contacts and obtained a list of builders across the ocean. I would need to sell the new home's twin to pay for the rest. I didn't tell Colin that one.

I still had the matter of acquiring citizenship. I thanked my Dad for that one as well. I dug around his boxed-up papers and found my birth certificate. He was already living in the west but kept my mother in London. After I arrived, he brought us both to join him. That little seemingly inconsequential decision planted the foundation for what came next.

It was four months before I received my registration papers for citizenship, another five before it was official. I secured the plot, called the contractors, and had the land surveyed. By the first month of the new year,

I received the call informing me of the exact dimensions of the property and where the house needed to be built. I wanted to verify the details and oversee the progress personally before the first brick was placed.

The contractor was a mammoth Irishman named Cameron Brimmicombe. I only assumed he was mammoth given the bass and volume of his voice over the phone. He knew my dad personally and recounted a tale from before I was born when he and my dad were rebuilding houses after the Belfast Bombing of 1972. Dad never told me that one. I faxed him the blueprints and Cameron recognized them as my dad's.

"I can't think of a better house to build," Cameron told me.

I didn't talk with Colin again. I didn't even try to contact him. I had Sushi one more time and said my goodbyes to James. He repeated his support.

The old house was priced competitively and sold quickly. My parent's lawyer handled the details. Since my father died, I had not been back.

Before I took the flight back to Scotland, I made one last visit to dad's grave. I touched the stone, which marked him and my mother's spot. I cried but I wasn't sure why. I missed them. That was true. Did I weep for the loss, about being alone? Was it because of events of my past, including my very birth, made the future practically paved before me. It could have been because I knew I would never see their graves again. I believed that was it.

*

It was a repeat of a year ago. Glasgow to Fort William, Fort William to Portree. I had a different bus driver who didn't say much. Cameron met me in Portree. He was six inches over six feet with a head topped with auburn. I stared at him for a full minute before he realized who I was.

"Mr. Weaver?" he asked. I nodded. He looked me over. "You must have a lot of your mother in ya."

"That's what people say," I responded. "Did you expect someone older?"

"No, I knew what to expect in that regard. I took the liberty of laying down property stakes and running ribbon around the border. I also put in the posts for the foundation, where the concrete goes for the patio and such."

"That's mighty kind of you, Cam." We shook hands. He led the way to his Vauxhall Astra. "So it's the same house your dad built that you just sold?" he asked.

"Yes."

"You born in it?"

"No," I answered, and then realized it wasn't exactly true, "well…kind of. It was basically the same house."

"Really?"

"He built variations on the same design. Few changes here and there, peach wood to burgundy, stuff like that."

He unlocked the door and I made for the driver's side.

"Going to drive now?" he asked.

I stopped, sighed, and walked around to the opposite door.

"Wrong country," I answered. We drove off.

"It odd, don't you think?" he said. "Building the same house over'n over."

"Dad was always odd. I thought you would know that."

"Your dad? Not in my experience. One of the most grounded, decent men I ever met."

I tried to remember my Dad being conventional, less irrational. Maybe when I walked home three miles from school because I hated the teacher. Or when I dropped his new casserole dish as I was removing it from the package.

Dad had asked if I had pressed the crosswalk buttons. When I told him I did, he let the matter drop and enrolled me in another school. When I broke the dish, he made me spend hours gluing the dozens of pieces back together before smashing it into the garbage and buying another. On both occasions, he didn't raise his voice or strike me.

"Different man to his son," I said.

"I knew him as a friend. No idea how he was as a father. He was the driver. I was the drinker."

"I'm following the lead of the man I knew."

"Funny how it led you back to me."

"Yeah...funny that."

*

"Got a name for them?" Cameron asked me as I stared at the three spear-tips at the top of the hill marking the north edge of the property. The car was parked off the road and we were standing in tall grass at the edge of the ribbon.

"Figured the locals would have named them," I answered.

"Aye, they did, they're exempt from the property claim. You can't touch 'em."

"Wasn't panning to."

He lifted the ribbon and I passed under it. We approached the stakes that marked the future house. Cameron waved and pointed his hand to mark the locations.

"So the patio here." He spun and moved his arms like he was directing traffic. "Which points the house that way with the terrace--"

"No," I interrupted, "terrace has to face the sea."

"But that means the main entrance faces the sea."

"Ok," I answered plainly.

"Well, I don't advise it. When we grade the road, we'll have to move around the house."

"Flip the garage, then. Pave a walk to the front."

"Flipping the garage would give you two front sides with no back," I answered with a shrug. "Just saying most everyone…meaning everyone, faces their main entrance to the road."

I walked across the plot until I stood where the main entrance would be. I imagined being twelve feet higher and seeing the shore of the cove.

"Yeah," I replied, "the terrace has to face the sea. I have to be able to see the cove from the terrace."

"Cove?" Cameron asked, sounding completely confounded, "What cove?"

"It's there," I replied as I walked into my imaginary study.

Cameron was looking around the field, seeing the stones and the cliffs. "Very well."

"So what do they call them?" I changed the topic.

"Pardon?"

I pointed to the spears. "The rocks? What do the locals call them?"

"*Li Ban*, *Fand*, and *Niamh*," he answered.

Those sounded familiar but I didn't know where from. "I'll have to look those up," I said. "When do we start?"

"When you give the word."

I inhaled a deep breath of moist spring air. "Mr. Scott," I joshed, "...the word is given."

"Scott?"

I cleared my throat. "Wrath of Kahn...Star Trek 2."

"I'm Irish."

"Couldn't help myself." I worked my way to the living room, beside the kitchen counters and the undivided dining hall. The entire area would be devoid of walls. "Anyways," I continued, "sooner the better."

"Where are you staying?"

"In Portree. B&B until the end of the month. Not sure where after."

I was navigating around nonexistent walls. Cameron crossed them to meet me. He joined me in the view of the scenery. "You must really like the view," he asked. "This plot must have been pricey."

"That it was."

"There are legal issues you'll need to settle."

"Yeah, I know. Permits for the wind turbine. Have to get a local lawyer to handle the details."

"Is this really worth it?"

I made for the rear exit. "To be perfectly honest with you...it's a bargain."

*

"Welcome back stranger," The server said.

"Pardon?" I asked.

Her hair and freckles were scarlet. Her cheeks were wide with a smile that showed both rows of teeth. She was rounded without being overweight. I was staying in the Coolin View again but had upgraded to a larger room that faced away from the sea.

I was alone in the early morning in the hotel dining hall. The novelty of the local food had worn off and I sat down with the intent of taking in eggs, bacon, and English muffins.

"You stayed with us last year," she said. I didn't remember from last time. Given her nature, I should have.

"Good memory," I answered.

"I try. You're the painter, I heard?"

"I didn't realize that was going around." I looked around the vacant room. "Didn't realize that was *worth* going around."

"More people can fit in Claggan Park than live here. Mother was talking. Word gets around, especially when they book a month."

She looked related to the owner of the hotel.

"Building a house north of here," I deadpanned my answer.

"Seem awfully young to settle."

"Well, I am."

She leaned in. "Don't misunderstand. Great place to settle. So what you paint?"

"Landscapes," I answered.

"Like here?"

I started wishing I had a newspaper to read. There wasn't even a menu. The tablemats were blank. "Yeah…few others, China, Argentina, Norway."

"Like the Seven Sisters Waterfall?"

Even that didn't rouse me. I shrugged. I was hungry and was expected at the plot. "Uh…yeah," I said.

"I love the Geirangerfjord. I went there was I was sixteen."

"Could I have tea with cream?" I said lethargically.

"Of course," she responded without a flinch. "So when am I going to see your Seven Sisters?"

"I sold it."

"Oh…Good money?"

"Not really, can I have a menu?"

"Oh…" she answered. I think that finally took the wind out of her sails. "Yes…of course." She brought one from an adjacent table that I could have reached myself.

"Thanks," I said.

"Well, holla when you're ready." She left for the kitchen.

I hadn't changed my mind on what to order.

*

YOU SOLD THE HOUSE?!!!!

That was Colin's last text message to me.

The virgin landscape was now populated by cement trucks, cargo vans, and a menacing crane that almost knocked over *Niamh*. I was looking at my cell phone and closed it without answering. Cameron was waving me over. He was standing next to a gentleman spearing the soil with an iron shaft.

"You see this," Cameron pointed down. "It's unstable."

"So," I answered, "pour some concrete in it.

"Just saying it will cost more."

"I got the payment for my old house. I'm plenty good."

"Walls go up by the end of the week. After the stone sets, it'll be smooth sailing. You got furnishings in mind?"

My attention was diverting to the passing tourist van negotiating the snaking road. I recognized it immediately.   "Suppose I'll have to do that, yeah," I said.

The bus slowed. Even from this distance away, I could see the fake wood paneling, the flaking blue finish. Through the window, I spotted the wild red hair of its driver. Five passengers inside were confused as to why their guide had stopped at this empty plot of land. Billy opened the door and stepped down as I approached close enough to hear him holler.

"William, my boy," he shouted.

"Billy my bus driver," I answered. "Was hoping I would find you." I approached and we shook hands. He had absolutely no regard for his passengers. They kept quiet and concerned in their seats.

"Hard to forget," he answered. "How long you here for?"

"Indefinitely," I answered, perking my left cheek as a smiled.

"Good on ya boy." He looked behind me and raised his brow. "Get away from all that madness elsewhere. Is that yours?"

"That is," I said.

He nodded and I could see him putting the thoughts together in his mind. "Might as well perch a cross on it. No greater symbol of faith I've never seen."

"No deities welcome here," I said. "No prayer. No piety. Only conviction."

"Well, one day, I'd like to meet your *betty*."

"One day, I hope you will. Thank you by the way."

"I've done nothing," he said sincerely.

"More than you know."

*

Five bedrooms. Three bathrooms. Two kitchens. There was a large Plasma TV that shared a ruckus room with a red futon. The dining room table had cherry and mahogany burl inlays, cherry veneers, and a hardwood core. Its eight chairs were hand crafted button tufted russet leather. My dad always thought big. I figured I would follow form.

The hardwood floors were couvertury maple. The kitchen countertop was black quartz. The walls were chestnut copper. The staircase was spiral. The bookshelves were Ikea.

I still didn't have a license to drive so the garage was empty. The ivory wind tower was some distance away, near the coast on the opposite side of the crescent cliffs. I made sure it could not be visible from any angle in the paintings. The cables ran underground to batteries under the house.

I filled the pantry some weeks back and only needed to head into town every two weeks. The wind turbine supplied adequate power but I had to be careful how many lights I left on. I wondered what I would do. How would I occupy my time? I wondered if I should paint. Occasionally, I would dream of the cove, of her. I posted a calendar on the stainless steel refrigerator and marked the date. I knew I wouldn't follow the cliché and mark off each day. I took a red marker, crossed off the year, and marked a new one, eight years and five months away.

I hung my paintings on empty walls where I found them. The view of the cove went in the kitchen. The cliffs were perched by the dining room table. The sitting stone and silhouette hung in a spare bedroom. The image of Skye was reserved for a prominent placement in the living room, across from the bay window.

I hadn't taken on a project in some months. Most of my reading was occupied by mythology, the regional folklore of the Hebrides and mainland Scotland. Some from Faroe as well. I chewed through the Fenian and Ulster Cycles. I looked up the legends of Li Ban, Fand, and Niamh. I read of kelpies, fairies, and the infestations of sea monsters that seemingly plagued every loch and lake in the region. I couldn't help but wonder if they were real as well.

*

"*Kiim-m-m...mer uh hae shiv*," I said to myself.   I rested upon the rose-colored sectional, looking out through the bay window to the sea. With the moon covered by clouds, the view was near black. I was reading up on the old language I heard her speak. Having never even learned a second tongue, it was proving extremely difficult for me.

"Hah guh mah tah-puh...leh-leh...eev." I wasn't very good at it. I found one I wanted to get right. *"Hah...geul...ah-kum orst-orst...orsht. Hah geul ah-kum orsht."*

It was past midnight when I heard a knock at the front door.

SIX

The fireplace in the living room was an electric model with a very convincing flame effect, so I had no firepoker to hold with conviction. There was no baseball bat and certainly no rifle. My best blade was a forged steak knife--not exactly matching the intimidation of a butcher's cleaver. I finally grabbed a Swiffer mop from the closet. I approached the rustic stained wooden door. I opened the iron-grilled speakeasy and looked out into the nebulous night. I bent my head around the view but saw nothing.

I held onto the Swiffer firmly. I unbolted the lock and opened the door. I peeked out from the periphery of the house and looked around the porch. I could hear the crashing waves, the distant whipping of the wind turbine.

"Who's out there?!" I shouted. It was nearly a half mile to the next house. The Swiffer was shaking. I closed the door quickly and began to lock the dead bolt.

There was another knock.

I threw the door open quickly, ready to strike with my thin plastic stick.

"HAH!" I shouted.

I looked down and saw him.

"Yes, I was here the first time," he said.

He stood barely up to my waist. He was bald with a bleached brow and beard. The hair was trimmed short only a few inches under his chin. His cavernous forehead ridges were that of an old man but his skin looked fresh and flush. He wore a gray robe that reminded me of a monk's. His was tied firmly around his waist. Bare feet my size were squeezed into sandals. I almost didn't notice his slightly oversized round ears.

My broom was still quivering.

"Who the hell are you?" I shouted.

"I know very well who I am," he answered with an accent flavored with a dash of Irish. "Do you know who you are?"

"What?" I snapped, weapon still at the ready. "This-This is my house. What are you doing here?"

"Wondering if you'll invite me in," he answered.

"Why the hell would I do that?"

"I don't know. I know I have to ask. But I don't know why you would say yes. We never ask why."

"Why?" I answered quickly. "Why." I rolled the word over in my mind. "You never ask why?" A small part of my brain was trying to understand what was occurring while another smaller part was screaming the other part to stop.

"No," he answered.

I lowered my weapon slowly. "Who are...what's your name?"

"MacGuffin."

"Seriously?"

"I'm rarely serious but in this case, yes."

"But that is—"

"Irish," he interrupted.

"I know that, it's also-"

"Are you wondering why?" he asked.

"I guess I shouldn't."

"We do have answers, just to not all the questions. We're incapable of asking the big ones, the ones you always ask. Even if you don't know the answer. The problem's with making the answer up." We stared a moment. "Still waiting for that invite."

I wondered if perhaps I was going crazy. I knew that if I convinced myself I was, that if I let that logical deduction settle in my mind, it would be an answer that would force him--and her--from the realm of possibility. I moved aside and leaned the broom against the sliding glass door that led to the coat closet. "Yes," I said slowly. "Please...come in."

He shuffled and squinted at the brightness of the entranceway. He spun, admiring every corner. "Well made," he said. "Old look, new build." He slipped off his sandals and placed them neatly next to my shoes. He took the initiative to walk down the hallway, ignoring the branches into bedrooms and bathrooms. He walked past the door to the ruckus room into the expanse that was the living room / dining room / kitchen. He climbed a stool on the opposite side of the kitchen counter. I walked around him and opened the cabinet to remove a glass. I figured I should offer a stein but I didn't have one.

"Don't have any spirits, do you?" he asked.

"No..."

"Too bad, been a long time. Stuck in the basement of an RBS for the past twenty years."

"RBS?" I asked.

"Royal Bank of Scotland. Thanks for the light, by the way?"

"Light?

"The fire...atop the house."

My head jolted alert. "The house is on FIRE?" I shouted as I made my way around the counter again.

He held a hand up. "Not in ways you can see or need to worry," he said

"What do you mean?"

"The beacon...the fire atop the house to show the way."

I was still elevated. "What beacon? What are you talking about?" I forced both my hands to grab the counter and I leaned in. "I'm sorry but what are you?"

"McGuffin."

"I know that," I snapped.

"McGuffin the Encourager," he announced proudly. "I'm a squat. Helpful spirit that aids people by offering clues to financial security."

"Never heard of you."

"We weren't all in the books, you know."

"And you were stuck in a bank?"

"Odd I know. In my prime, I would help farmers, hunters, business owners. Giving items or ideas to encourage them to find the answer they always sought in life."

I had no idea where the origin of the name came from but I was pretty sure it wasn't him. "And was McGuffin always your name?" I asked.

"No...one time I was called *Haltija*. You'll have to settle for Guff. Seriously, no beer?"

"I don't drink. Why," I stopped myself. This was getting frustrating. "Dammit...this house is a beacon?"

"Yes...I could ask you why. You would have to know of us...know...not believe. We're not about that."

I nodded and sat atop the counter, the glass still in my hand. "I do know," I said. "Everything I've done was because I know."

"If you want to welcome us, you'll have to forgo the logic of your normal world. You did this irrationally. You did it because of something which didn't make sense." I could tell Guff was putting it together. "...or someone."

"Yes," I revealed.

Guff nodded and pouted his lips. "How fortunate you must have been."

I glanced at the glass in my hand. I lifted it between us.

"I have apple juice," I said.

"Why not," he said with shrug.

I opened the stainless steel refrigerator and removed the carton. "So you were drawn here?" I asked.

"Like a moth," he explained. "But this light does not burn, it nourishes." I offered him the full glass. "Once was a time when shade was the shortage. The light faded every year...until it was gone. I'd bless you if I was pious." He began to drink slowly.

"Are you hungry?" I asked.

He swallowed and gasped agreeably. "Grains and nuts only for me," he said.

"That's specific," I said.

"Always is," Guff responded.

I opened the pantry and fished around my selection. I pulled out a sealed cereal box.

"Granola good?" I asked.

"Yes please," he said.

I offered him the bowl and poured the cereal to the top.

"Milk?" I asked.

"Can't," Guff said.

"Another rule?"

"No...Lactose."

"Ah."

I grabbed my own glass and filled it. I nibbled the granola directly from the box. Guff tossed the clusters into this mouth and chewed them slowly, savoring every crunch. He closed his eyes and rolled his head as he took the longest time to swallow. Then he repeated with the next mouthful. I wasn't sure I wanted to bother him. He obviously had been starved of such luxury for many years. It was by the third swallow that I finally broke the silence.

"So what now?" I asked.

"Who was it?" he diverted.

"She called herself Skye."

"Here?"

I pointed with my chin to the front exit. "The cove out there," I said. "You can't see it until you reach the cliffs, or unless you're on the second floor."

"I know of it. Let me guess, a pleasant sequence of coincidences and happy accidents?" He grabbed another handful.

"Yes," I said. "I painted her. Like it was--"

"Fate?" Guff interrupted. He shook his head. "Fate involves order...a plan. Only luck here." He pointed a crooked finger to me. "And don't look any further into it."

I nodded. Luck and chance. Nothing written. Impossible events simply occur because they can't.

"So you have rules...random and specific," I said.

"Exactly."

"And you're all different?"

"Each unique, with our own convention to answer for. Your kind would see one...and that one would equate a people. Still only one."

"So a story about mermaids...it was always one mermaid."

"Something to that," he spoke through his open mouth. "More to it-- mermaids, syrens, amabie, narissa--dozens, hundreds, all different. Some got fish in 'em, others squid, dolphin, little bits of many. Some you'd trade your soul for a kiss. Others with faces to haunt your dreams until life took sympathy and killed ya'." He was staring out through the back window. He was remembering those from distant memories, the angelic and the demonic, the magnificent and the monstrous.

"And Skye...the selkie," I said, jostling Guff from his diversion. "She's only one..."

"Only one with her convention," he said. I was confused by the word as he said it again, *convention*. I would know the word later as the set of commandments each of them had to follow, which defined their very existence. "There are others close to her," Guff explained as he pushed the empty bowl to me, "related but different. One can take form at a whim while another is set by a clock. Some are wicked while are others enchanting. Some hoard, others share. Hanging under bridges with relatives prowling in attics."

Guff hadn't carried a conversation of significant length with anyone since World War II. His convention didn't prohibit him from explaining things unlike so many others of his kind. He had wanted such an exchange for a long time. I offered him another glass of juice and he gladly accepted.

"We counted a million million in our prime," he explained as I cleaned up, loading dishes and closing doors. "Your stories never touched more than a tenth of what lived. Now you never will. Most faded without a single legend accounting for them. I weep for Sylfaen of the Crooked Creeks, the Thornwarden of Dense Forests, and the Cancer Hound of Foul Clouds." He held those names close to him and he broke his speech to respect them. "Meanwhile you spin a thousand yarns of winged faeries and mermaids." Some creatures would never have a story told. Like trees falling in the forest, do they still make a sound?

"And there was never a legend of you?" I asked. "You have a family?" I circled the kitchen counter and joined Guff on his side. The power saver kicked in and dimmed the lights. I noticed a slight glimmer to Guff's eyes, a silvery sheen like the ones observed in dogs.

"I'm a squat brother of Oggrak--the one who bites off the maidenhead of sea vessels," Guff said, "and the son of Moesa, the nymph of falling snow." He stopped and drew in a lungful. "She didn't last long. Not much magic left in Switzerland."

"Your father?" I asked.

"Like many, a man. A tourist taking in the hills, saved from an avalanche because a fixation on a short tree fooled him to thinking it was woman dressed head to toe in white furs. Turns out she was. She saw him seeing and knowing her. She bent the snow over and froze a dwelling he could never leave. Easy choice...remain with the angel and never wish for more or allow the snow to crush you. He never saw hunger and never knew a chill. I was the fruit of it."

"How long ago?"

"During your first great gun war. I don't count days or months. Father was a great man. He was wise. Smart enough to tell me nothing of your world. Knew better."

There was an unfortunate realization I had difficulty avoiding. To explain it would be to empower it. To prove it would be to justify it. "My...friend," I paused as I wondered if it were true, "Colin, wouldn't be able to handle it. He's the rational one. The principle of not asking is against his character. He would say that the blind acceptance without questioning is a religious tenet."

"RELIGION," Guff coughed out, drops of spit hitting the counter, "Bah! Organized nonsense." He pointed firmly at me. "As much their fault as anything else. Killed us quite well enough until science perfected the process. That was the first of it. The marker of madness to come. It began when you made all the stories touch. They had to make sense to one another. Then you wove your fingers and made up gods to explain it all." Guff dropped off his stool and navigating the large open area, steering around the dining table and making his way to the couches that sat before the artificial fire.

"Then many gods became few gods," he continued, "You make sense of it. The elements were living, then dead, then worse, made up of smaller things of lesser worth."

"Was mankind part of that?" I asked. "Were we as you until we defined ourselves?"

"I never knew...mother never told. The moment we ask is the moment the answers become real. So don't know. Maybe an elf and a sea lord coupled and had children that asked too many questions too often."

It was one thing to accept Skye and Guff, but all the myths and monsters I grew up with? Was Loch Ness an unexplained creature that suffered a needless death when we insisted it didn't exist? Were mermaids captivating angels of the sea until mutated by science into manatees?

"You had it all, you know?" Guff continued. "Dragons, harpies, faeries...then you had to bring your logic. Had to say what couldn't be. Found your physics, found your chemistry. Created the answers which gave you control over it.

"You're saying we created science? Retroactively?"

Guff nodded. "Big word," he replied sarcastically, "happy you said it?"

I sudden comprehension came to me. "That would make our world the fantasy...assuming there's a reality to compare it."

"Shades of gray, I see it."

"Without logic to explain it, we turn to the absurd. But even without religion, wouldn't god still be an explanation?"

"If there was one...but there isn't."

"But without science or God, there's no origin. That can't be. Has to be a reason."

"Why?" Guff leaned in. "Why must you ask?"

"My people are compelled to ask. Some consider it a strength."

"That I'm sure it is. Built your cars, your washing machines, your factories. Took this world in ways we never could...fighting a battle we've no hope to win. Always thought your people did it intentionally. I think now you didn't know better. If you did, you wouldn't still tell our stories.

"Those tales caused damage as well, as they began justifying our existence by connecting us with others. Like that bastard Heinrich Kramer. All his stories and all his ideas, explaining things he shouldn't. Superstition didn't help. It's no wonder the only ones to survive to this time are the ones you never heard about or got many of the stories wrong. The kind like Eilean of Skye, Banya of Open Ocean, and Huldar the Covered One is so precious. Only by their strength of soul did they persevere."

"Eilean of Skye?" I asked. "Is that what you call her?"

"I choose whichever one comes to mind first. If she wishes Skye, then that's what you will use."

*

I looked at the gold painted clock on the wall as it ticked past two in the morning. My eyes were getting heavy. Guff had shown no signs of tiring. I assumed that was normal.

"So I imagine you'll want to stay," I stated more than asked. I groaned, struggling to stand.

"If you'll have me?" Guff answered.

I stretched my neck and took a moment to wonder if the last few hours had been a bizarre dream. Maybe I was still sitting by the bay window, passed out with a book of Gaelic mythology resting on my chest.

"You have rules about personal property?" I asked him.

"I wouldn't be a very good helpful squat if I stole from those I helped."

"You could be lying. You could be a vampire or something."

"What you called vampires we called ghulath and they died out two hundred years ago."

"Still, you could have rules you're forbidden to tell me. Perhaps you're actually a curse I've fooled myself into taking in."

"I guess it is all about trust. Why did you allow me into your home?"

I looked about the room. All those years to wait. How long before I grew tired of waiting? How long before the memory of the cove grew blurry with time?

"I think I rather enjoy the idea of having company such as you…curse or blessing." I turned and approached the door to the ruckus room. "So we'll give it the evening. Here's hoping I won't wake up tied to the bed with you morphed into looking like me." I opened the door and turned to Guff, still standing by the fake fireplace.

"I don't sleep," he said.

"Not even to rest? There's a futon."

"It's appreciated," Guff answered.

I moved to the stairs. Cognitive thought was failing. Sentences were not forming complete in my head. I took a few steps, then returned and poked my head out.

"Guff, did your father ever see the outside world again?"

"Nope…never did. He never asked to either."

I nodded. "You never asked my name."

"I knew your name the moment I entered your home, William Weaver."

*

I woke up to the smell of lemony fresh pine floor cleaner. It was pervasive. The hardwood was reflective and slick. My wool socks were precarious. I braced at the precipice and looked down the glossy steps. It would be like slipping on ice eighteen times. I took off the socks.

I found Guff in the center of the living room, standing on my glass coffee table. Eyes closed, he was pushing the air with open palms. He bent a knee and balanced himself deftly with one foot. He slowly rotated his arms around his waist and turned his palms inward. He brought his hanging foot back down, bent both knees, and pulled his elbows close to his body.

"Guff?" I asked.

"Yes, William."

"Are you doing Tai Chi?"

"Sun style," he answered. "Something wrong with that?"

"Not exactly. Just not something I expected to see. You hungry?"

"I'll eat if offered."

I repeated the preparation from last night. Granola with no milk. I added extra oats to his, sliced apple to mine. Guff joined after his routine had been completed.

"Guff," I said, "I was meaning to ask you something... something you should be able to answer." He nodded to encourage after accepting the bowl. "How did your kind vanish? I mean did you become human, fade away, or did you change into something science could explain?" I added milk to my bowl.

"Not so graceful. Not so quietly. Our fate was left to *demons*."

I looked up from the pouring milk and hung on the last word heard. I stumbled and pulled up the carton before it overflowed the bowl. "Demons?" I asked.

"The division between noegic and magic, like rubbing your hands together." He acted out what he said, a clump of granola between his palms. He then held out the cluster between his fingers. "What forms between is a demon. Formed from us but working for you. Hypocrites." He devoured the mouthful. "Can't fault 'em too much. They're obeying their convention, as they should. Your rules became law, and the demons came marching on our turf, forcing us away, and killing most. They'll be the last to go. Wonder what they'll think when it's their names on the bill and go about killing themselves?"

"So just the small ones left?"

"Squats mostly. The ones that can hide. Kinda Like your dinosaurs..." Guff pauses and coughed a laugh as he swallowed a mouthful. "Heh...bloody dinosaurs. Few big ones left."

"You said *neogic*. What's that?" I asked with a spoon in my mouth. "I figured logic was the mirror to magic."

"Logic doesn't spread out. It can't grow or influence. It just is. Noegic is the force that enforces your logic. It's your will to organize, put down rules you need to follow. Noegic is the twin, the mirror."

"Yin-Yang." I said.

"Just as long as you know there's no evil with either. Just how it is."

"Magic radiates from you. Noegic radiates from us. The more you talk about it, the more it sounds like we're living in a dream."

"No less than when we shared the world with you on equal standing. I can see the argument of wanting sense in your life. To sail the seas and be unafraid of a siren song. To cross a bridge and not worry about an unspoken toll. Keep your children safe from goblins. In order to survive, you passed customs and superstitions and we lived peacefully for thousands of years... until you finally figured you didn't need to accommodate."

Guff finished his meal first and pushed the bowl to my side. I placed mine over his and let them fall into the sink.

"So could I hurt you by quoting quadratic formulas?"

"I'd prefer you didn't but I'm not sure it would have an effect. All your kind did was rationalize. Offer something that didn't include us. Perhaps you smelled something foul that made you see things. Maybe something gone broke in your brain. Some pill popped causes some chemical unbalance. You catch us on a camera and discount it as a hoax."

I looked around the house, at the few paintings on the wall. "This place...it was because of her. Because I followed something that was irrational to a place I shouldn't have been, to meet someone that shouldn't exist. Logic would offer something simple, something sensible. Something my friend Colin would accept. I never considered it a possibility. Even now, can I trust my own memories?" I waited even though I knew he wouldn't answer. He didn't. "I guess I don't care...as long as I don't doubt what happened..."

"I hold hope you won't," Guff said. He dismounted the stool and sauntered to the entrance. "This beacon is all we got."

I nodded, and then I realized what he said. "Wait, we?"

I heard a knock at the door. I raced quickly around the kitchen counter after Guff as he waited by the entrance. He didn't open it but was expecting me to. He nudged a chin to the door. I stared at the wood a moment, wondering what waited beyond it.

It thumped again, lower to the ground, lower than even Guff. Knowing the random assortment of legends running through my head, it could be anything. It was odd that I immediately considered the most outlandish possibility. My initial assumptions were of a troll or a goblin or some talking animal. The likelihood of it being Cameron or Billy was not the foremost on my mind.

I trembled as I opened the door. I didn't have my Swiffer with me.

"Guffin!" the midget shouted in a slightly squeaky voice.

"Percival," Guff answered. The new arrival was half Guff's height with stumpy limbs and a smile that reached ear to ear. His head rocked as he opened his oversized mouth to talk. If I were seeing him on television, I would dismiss him as a well-controlled muppet. His skin was patterned like one. Eyes were large. All he wore was a red knit turtleneck and rope tied blue trousers.

I found myself trying to place which Henson creation he resembled.

"Weaver William," Guff continued, "this is Percival, half brother."

"Ernie," I muttered. That was the one.

"No, Percival," Guff corrected.

"Cousin?" I asked.

"Same mother," Percival said. "Father was a hermit dwarf."

I moved aside and exposed the entranceway. "I suppose I should let you in as well." As I turned my head, I noticed from the corner of my eye Percival shifting to resemble the silhouette of a full-grown man. He lost all detail and became a shadow, nearly amorphous. I jerked my head back and found the squat looking up to me again.

"Wait," I said. "What the hell was that?"

"Percy is the ghost in the side of your eye," Guff replied, "vanishing as you turn."

"Never got anything for doing that," Percival said.

"Would it hurt to do something with it, other than frightening people?"

I still wasn't sure what I was expected to do. I understood the house was a beacon. What would it attract?

"I don't have a lot of rooms here," I said.

"I just need a corner," Percival answered. "Some place you pass but seldom look. I'll make well there."

I moved aside and allowed him to enter.

"Welcome then, I said. "I assume you'll behave." He held out his three-fingered hand and we shook on it. He brought in nothing with him. He took note of the placement of the lights and the shadows they made. He nodded, satisfied. Guff was still standing next to me as I closed the heavy door.

A loud thud nearly cracked the wood. The knock came from over my head. I turned and gave Guff a look that easily conveyed *who is this*.

"Get used to that," Guff answered.

Without even a moment's further trepidation, I unlatched and swung open the door.

The wolf had grey black fur that blended well against the cloudy sky behind it. Its eyes were beaming silver, almost like chrome. It was twenty feet long and had no hope of even fitting through my front door. Its incisors were the size of my head and were only a few feet from it.

"Hi," I said forcefully.

SEVEN

A diminutive winged faerie with oversized tulip petals for ears and fine grass for hair fluttered inches from my head. I awoke, staring at her light green within dark green eyes.

"William?" she squeaked. "Morning to you. Don't be blue."

"Hello Miran," I groaned. "You were…almost overdue."

"We have new arrivals this day. What will you say?"

I scratched my growing goatee. "Plural? Squats? I'm sure they can stay."

She darted closer and perched herself upon my scruffy chin. "A faelan, a dawnling, and another I don't know. Now don't be slow."

"Of course not," I moaned. "Now go."

Miran is Playful was responsible for the vast majority of myths related to similar faeries. She loved to travel. With her speed, she had crossed the planet many times. I also believed she was borderline psychotic. The last time I didn't answer with a rhyme, she stuck me in the leg with her half-inch sword. I pushed myself from the bed as she raced under the door to return downstairs. I considered installing a runner board to stop her from doing that.

I still wasn't sure why I said yes to Guff, Percy, Geraz, Miran and Izee. Guff promised more would come in time. It never occurred to me to reject them. If this home was the last refuge they had, to deny entry would be to kill them. They probably wouldn't leave regardless. I could imagine a therapist diagnosing me as schizophrenic. That enough would drive them from my home. I would have considered it if I suspected I was hallucinating. I didn't care if I was some sad character stuck in a *Terry Gilliam* movie. Every sensation was alive and telling me my lack of doubt was gospel.

*

Izee the Curious was already helping himself to a cut of Gorgonzola I had kept under plastic wrap on the counter. It was only when the rat stood on his hind legs did he reveal his articulate fingers. He held onto the cheese with one hand as I passed him.

"*Guten morgen, Bauer*," he shouted in his native tongue.

"Morning 'Zee," I answered. "Please remember to keep the cheese covered."

"*Ratten sind überlegen! Wir vergessen nie!*" he shouted. Only Guff knew German but seldom translated. He said it wasn't worth me knowing. Izee felt superior to all others, including me and the other fae of the house. I had no idea why he refused to speak any other language.

He and Guff were one of the few that actually needed to eat, even though they did so infrequently. Percival stayed in the corner, scaring me occasionally as I entered the room. After a week had passed, I barely took notice. Izee and Miran arrived a few days after.

Geraz the Wolf never spoke, never growled, and was more or less a wimp. He was also insubstantial unless you looked directly in his eyes. He slept most of the day in front of the garage and only stretched his legs out at night.

Guff was washing the patio windows.

"What are you doing?" I asked

"Come to thinking I might help out," Guff answered.

"That's thoughtful."

He put down the watered glass cleaner and squeegee. "I could coordinate. Make sure everyone behaves. Remind you occasionally of the good you're doing."

He followed me to the front entrance. "It will depend on how many show up," I said. "It's one thing for demented faeries and talking nazi mice—"

"*Ratte*!" Izee said with surprising volume behind us.

"Any more like Geraz," I continued, "and I won't be able to accommodate. Not even taking into account how I'll afford it."

"They will pay," Guff said as we reached the door. "I'll make sure of it. Miran brought gold."

"Which the banks won't take."

"Percy offered shiny pebbles."

"Good for the garden and not much else. Do you know who's here?"

"You sure you wish to greet them now?"

"Rude of us to make them wait." I didn't bother looking through the speakeasy and just swung the door open wide. After nearly stepping on Izee on his arrival, I remembered to look carefully around the entrance before stepping out. I initially counted two, but then noticed the third.

She had cricket legs and a carapace that looked like an evening gown. Tiny antennae poked from spider silk hair. She held a flower stalk like a spear in her hands. She was the smallest one yet.

"I don't know you," Guff said with a huff.

"*Pixis of Fruitful Soil*," she answered in an accent I found out later was from New Zealand.

"Your convention?" he asked.

"Among many, I must always touch natural soil. You have a garden?"

"No," I answered, "not even potted plants."

"Oh no," she said, disheartened.

"We can fix that," I said.

She lit up. "That would be salvation. Until then, I will force the flowers in the field to bloom."

"Got coins?" Guff asked, assuming his assumed role with conviction. I patted him on the shoulder.

"Blooming flowers is more than adequate," I said. "They can all pay in their own way." Pixis bounded into the uncut fields around the house. I could track her movement by the sudden purple blossoms sprouting in winding lines around the house. I wouldn't see her again for another week. Guff and I turned our attention to the large rusty red fox with nine tails standing next to the patient, tongue-hanging, soft-coated wheaton terrier. Guff addressed the fox.

"And you?" he snapped.

The fox unfurled its tails like a peacock. They could reach tip to tip from my outspread arms. The fox sat and straightened its front legs to push its body up.

"Her name is Inari of Nine Tails," I said as I heard her whisper in my head. "You're the last of the Nippon. Come in." The fox walked slowly into the house.

I was still staring at her as Guff turned to address the dog.

"And you?" Guff asked. "What's your convention?" The dog tilted its head and closed its mouth to swallow. "Come on," he persisted, "out with it!"

The dog let out an exuberant bark.

Guff shrugged. "You're actually just a dog, aren't you?" he said. I turned to reenter the house. This was not a pet sanctuary.

"Go," Guff shooed him away. "Go on. Come back when you develop language!"

*

"I'll offer to handle the affairs of payment," Guff continued. "Ensure they pay in wood for fire, wind for your fans, rain for crops, sun for comfort and storms to wash away a foul mood…because storms always make me feel better."

"Me too," I said. It was dinner and like the days before, Guff and I sat across the massive dining table. Izee rested atop his plate to my right, Miran settled among the fruit in the centerpiece. "Thunder and lightning," I added.

"Different people," Guff answered, "both known well." He swallowed a spoonful of grains.

"And no on the wood. That fireplace is fake."

"I know it's fake, I have been here for three weeks. It's always good to have wood for fire."

"Guess you have a point."

"And do you require comfort?"

I stopped the forkful of penne with parmesan in béchamel sauce inches from my mouth. I put the utensil back on the plate.

"Comfort?" I asked.

"Nymph, Neirid, Narf. Most still around, making rounds with mortal men. Short affairs and vacation flings. No ties or dependencies. That lucky chap who counts his stars for the blessing. They vanish without thanks or worse, a fond kiss and a farewell to stain all future loves. Hate it when they do that. Soils a man's expectations for the rest of his days."

"This is not a brothel, Guff," I said.

"No money traded, lad. You said pay in their own way and this is their currency. They have nothing else to tender. If we keep this rule paramount, they must recompense."

"No," I answered. "There is no compulsory payment. Volunteer only. If they will be so gracious, they will pay...NOT in a bed though. Not in that way. Those are welcome without fee." I pointed with the fork. "Stress that Guff."

"Aye, Weaver. You fond of holding that torch?"

"Soils a man's expectations for the rest of his days, right? Thankfully, I don't have to wait *that* long"

"How many years remain?"

"Eight."

"You might be likely to forget such a tryst in that time."

I took a moment to slowly chew the pasta and savor the sauce and texture. "If I am to remain true to why this house was built," I said finally, "to maintain this, then I must remain loyal."

"I understand now, lad. You think of her and us. I will never bring it up again. If you change your mind, though, I will not condemn and shall look the other way."

Izee noticed first and lifted his head. Guff and I turned in unison as Inari entered. Her face was smooth with not a wrinkle or crease on her skin. Sharp dark eyebrows sat over almond-shaped hazelnut eyes. Her complexion was fair and without blush. As she looked at me, the curves of her nose all but vanished. Her visible age was impossible to guess. She looked twenty-five or forty-five. As she turned to walk around the chair, I noticed her high cheeks. My attention quickly shifted to the single tail sticking out from behind the white robe she borrowed from the shower.

Her hair matched that of the solitary tail. She was far larger than a fox. She was not like Skye, emerging from an outer layer. She kept everything inside save for that one tail.

She took the seat to my left. Miran was not amused at the diversion. She continued to brood in the centerpiece.

"Inari," I greeted.

"They call you the Weaver," Inari said. Her voice was elegant, soft but rich with deep tones. She had picked up English long ago but it was still not her first tongue. She spoke every word as if it was its own sentence.

"Just William," I said. "Too many Weavers to just single me out."

Miran yelled from the fruit, "We already single you out! There is no doubt!"

"Thank you, Miran," I said. "Now don't shout."

Inari bowed her head nearly to the plate. "Thank you for our salvation."

"It wasn't my intention to create it. It was, as everything is, an accident, but a pleasant one I'm quickly discovering. Do you eat?" She nodded. "What's your preference? I'll see to it."

"Fruit like you have will be adequate. I can see to my own needs."

"What's your preference?" I repeated.

Her smile was slow to form and she bowed again. "Dates and figs."

"I'll see to it."

"I was close to fading. I lost my home. My children and generations after had forgotten me. I feared our old shelters had fallen to ruin."

"This isn't an old home. It's new."

"*Nicht genug Löcher,*" Izee interjected.

Inari straightened her back and looked at me. I noticed Guff giving me a dead stare.

"You have hopeful eyes," Inari whispered.

"And yours are sad," I replied.

She nodded. Her head moved a lot but her arms were kept tight at her sides. "I was close to standing ground and letting the demons send me off."

"You are an elder," Guff said, finally entering the conversation. "Thought your like was extinct?"

She turned to Guff. "I remained to track my lineage," she answered, "despite being forsaken."

"Their loss. How many bridges do you have?"

"Fifteen scattered in the wind. Barely a drop of me left in them after so long."

"Bridges?" I asked.

"What we call our human children," Guff explained. He returned to Inari. "When I first saw you, I must admit, I thought you were Jade Jing."

"Jade Jing?" I asked.

Guff opened his mouth to answer but Inari turned to address me. "A relative that possessed women. Instead of taking shape, she compelled them to engage in…acts on her behalf. Manipulation and deception was the order of her convention."

Morality began and ended with whichever lover she took. I mourn her passing. I do not wish her return."

She reached across to the centerpiece and took an apple. I offered her my unstained knife. As she accepted it, I noticed her long fingernails.

"Why such a house, then?" she asked. "So grand, if not for us?"

"It was my father's," I replied. "I didn't consider anything less. So you would be kitsune?"

"Not entirely."

Guff interjected, "The legends rarely got them perfect."

"*Unsere Legenden sind von höchster Lager!*" Izee snapped. I glanced at Guff to translate. He shook his head.

"That I believe," I said.

"Some were more accurate than others," Guff said. "The ones that matched perfectly were the first to fade."

"How many you think are left?" I waited for my guests to answer. Inari looked down to her lap like a scolded child. Guff glanced at the ceiling. "I suppose then," I answered for them, "we'll just have to hope and wait."

A moment passed before Miran spoke up from atop a banana. "So we stay? What luck. You might even get to—"

"DON'T…finish…that…rhyme," I snapped.

"Humph," she replied.

She was going to stab me later. I was sure of that.

*

I had improperly assumed the faelin, dawnlings, squats, and faeries that were arriving carried a history of centuries with them. In truth, most were generations past ancestors that founded the most famous tales. Izee was the last of an extended line of talking rodents that once included squirrels, porcupines, and chipmunks. For many decades, it was he and a French Canadian vole named Vincent. Izee lost his cheerful demeanor after surviving the bombing of Dresden in 1945. He was only 105 years old.

I could only imagine the alien personality emerging from a soul ten times older. As Guff explained it, squats and by assumption all of his kind, could recall every moment of their existence as if reliving it. Every death would carry its impact no matter the decades or centuries that passed.

Inari was over a thousand years old.

As we shared the meal and the evening, she opened up about her experiences and the others of her kind that had not survived.

She spoke of Nytsia Mamuna, an eastern animal spirit that patrolled dark forests. She wasn't one wolf but three, which merged to create her human side. They could shift positions and the dominant one forming her body would control her disposition, from kind to malevolent. Her look could also change depending on the dominant wolf. She had been mistaken for nearly a dozen different myths across Russia and Eastern Europe. She faded in 1755.

Prana of Short Breath was another wolf spirit. She assumed a female body to draw the breath and life energy from her victims. She had no redeeming qualities. She was killed in 1911.

Harmay the Snake was a large reptile that could shed her skin and reveal herself as a large bird with a human face. She was a seductress in both forms. As the bird, she would lure mortals with her song and force them to act against their nature. As a snake, she could invade the dreams of men, appearing as a beautiful woman. She would seduce and drain their life. Inari had not heard from Harmay since 1875.

Tennyo Myogoki was a Japanese fairy and personal acquaintance of Inari. Unlike Miran, Tennyo could move from diminutive flyer to adult human. The demons claimed her at a Hokkaido farm in 1945. Her passing left Inari alone. None of her culturally- or blood-bound fairy relatives made it into the nuclear age.

I couldn't help but be attracted to Inari. There was a manner about her. I felt I was admiring royalty in some way. It was the kind of distant admiration one reserved for a governess or, given the modern age, an attractive highschool teacher. Like that, I placed Inari in that position, well enough away from the realm of possibility. In these years, the image of Skye had never left. I could recall that kiss and the taste of salt water would roll across my tongue. The dream was not under threat.

*

"The painting hanging across from the front window," Inari asked me, "Your love?"

"Whom I hope will reciprocate," I replied.

I was leading her to one of the spare bedrooms I had made up weeks prior. It was on the main floor, next to a bathroom, and was the largest spare I had.

"You'll need something to wear," I continued, "more…appropriate than my robe. Would a kosode suffice?"

Inari was impressed. "And you have one?" she asked.

"Not yet, but I'll go into town tomorrow and order one."

"I will admit a weakness for selfless kindness," Inari said matter-of-factly. "If she would not return, I would have considered taking you."

I stopped and turned slowly. I felt a billiard ball wedge in my throat.

"W-Well-Well…Well. Thank…you?"

"But it is already too late. I can never reveal my true form to a lover, which you have already seen. If so, I would be forced to depart. As well it is. My last proved too great a loss. I refused human contact since."

I fumbled with the spare door and offered her the key.

"This is yours for as long as you wish," I muttered.

"Thank you, William," she said softly. She entered the room and I stood in front of the closed door for a good minute before returning to the waiting Guff in the living room. He didn't offer a smile or a scold.

We shared a blank moment before he finally said, "I won't condemn and shall look the other--"

"No," I interrupted politely before leaving for bed.

EIGHT

I never drank alcohol but made an exception for my 24th birthday. I purchased a tall bottle of 20-year old single malt Talisker Scotch whisky. It made an impression. Only Izee, Guff, and I drank. Inari enjoyed her figs while Pixis nibbled on leaves in her potted plant in the corner. Miran couldn't be bothered to care and Percival was invisible and content in the corner. Kareen made *kaab el ghzal* for dessert, which resembled crusty green turds wrapped in phyllo pastry. It was actually crushed almonds, another example of the unusual cuisine I had gotten used to with Kareen's arrival.

If it wasn't for his talents, I could never have placed Kareen as another departure from the ordinary world. He was average height. He had normal ears and normal eyes. He was hairless and wore a pristine white cotton suit that emphasized his ebony skin. He also radiated a bouquet of cumin, coriander and cinnamon. When we initially shook hands, mine smelled of ginger for two days. This carried into the food he prepared. Suddenly, every dish bore the mark of some distant country I had no hope in visiting. With the slightest brush of his fingers, like a skilled illusionist, Kareen could muster any spice harvested anywhere on Earth.

Paprika, coriander, and cardamom were his personal favorites. He only needed to open his hands and his cupped palms would be full of seeds. On special occasions, he could even muster up a bushel of saffron.

Although he could smile, we never heard Kareen speak. We gathered his name from Inari. The only other features of his convention I was able to figure out was that he drank salted water and that on the spring and fall equinoxes, he needed to be buried up to his head in the garden. This was in addition to an apparent compulsion to make my house smell like an Indian restaurant.

In the past two years, the only other arrival had been Marik the Sitting One—-a squat known to Guff who specialized in giving people nightmares by sitting on them while they slept. He fed on the disturbance, devouring the fear and wiping the memory of the encounter. I began locking the door to my bedroom. He barely spoke and at this late hour was prowling the neighboring houses for a victim.

I heard a knock and everyone stopped and straightened their backs. Normal people don't knock at 11:00 pm. I wiped the drink from my lips and meandered to the door as carefully as possible. I opened the speakeasy and saw nothing. No clouds or water. I then noticed the pale emaciated fingers ending in sharpened fingernails.

"Guff!" I shouted back to the dinner table. Guff dismounted his chair and hobbled to meet me. I whispered as he got close, "Can demons enter this house?"

"No," Guff answered, "unless you are starting to have doubts—"

"Of course not," I whispered. Inari and Kareen approached us.

"Then he cannot," Guff said. "They reside in noegic."

I inhaled my trepidation. I swallowed my fear. I unlocked and slowly opened the door. The figure was stretched over eight feet. He looked like a four-limbed human harvester spider, with long pencil-thin legs connected to a small torso. His fingers were equally stretched, as was his neck, connected to a head that bent below his shoulders to look at me.

There was an unnatural shadow enveloping him. It covered the details of his body and muffled his face save for a thin mouth sprouting fangs and red eyes that blinked out of unison. I was instantly terrified but the fear was not from a survival instinct. It was a childish fear, something basic that I had forgotten. It was a fear of under the bed, of in the closet, of all the places I was told not to go.

"Lows!" Guff shouted in disgust. "This place is not welcome to you."

Lows' voice was unsettling. It was deep and gargled. When he talked, I never saw lips closing over his teeth. When he paused, a black tongue flicked into view and licked around his mouth like he was always thirsty. "I assumed…it was welcome to all."

Guff kept his stance, which fortified my feet to remain where they were. "Not you," he said, "or any others of your kind."

"Is this a demon?" I asked.

"I am…no…demon!"

Guff kept his eyes on Lows but addressed me. "Lows of Lakesides. More rodent than even Izee."

"You're fae then?" I asked Lows.

"Where is Bungar the Wicked One," Guff asked, "or the Cancer Hound of Foul Clouds. Are they coming now to?"

"Taken by the fade…long ago," Lows growled. "I mourn them… though you won't."

"That's right," Guff snapped.

"Guff, enough," I interjected. I stepped in front of him. Every inch closer brought an increasing panic that I would begin to see details through the shadow. "Why are you a threat?"

"I am…no threat…to you," Lows answered.

"Nonsense," snapped Guff. "You can't make sense of his words. There is no treaty or mutual agreement. His convention can never be suppressed. It is a compulsion none can deny, regardless of salvation. He can take to feral dog or oversized rat. Don't invite him in."

I looked at Guff's committed posture, then to the others at the other end of the hallway. Miran had appeared. She obviously didn't want the likes of Lows in the house either. Kareen wasn't smiling but I could tell he wasn't concerned. I could read Inari's expression, as I always could without her words.

"Am I to assume," I asked Lows, "you're nothing short of the boogeyman? You want a bed to hide under?"

"I am…bound to darkness," Lows growled. "It need not be…in a closet…or where you…sleep."

"Don't consider it," Guff demanded.

"William," Inari spoke to me but addressed Guff and the others that agreed with him, "Guff is correct in many ways, but I feel his emotions have unbalanced him. Are we to begin to refuse?"

I looked to Guff, still resolute.

"From what I know," I said to Lows, "Guff is correct in your compulsion. If it told you to destroy this place, you would, despite regrets."

"That is…correct," Lows answered.

"See?" Guff interjected. "He is *Barghest. Bunyip.*

"But wouldn't those creatures be dead, explained away, like all the other old myths?"

"For some strange reason types like him always seem to stick around. Just the same, don't permit entry. He will bring only fear."

"I will...not...enter," Lows said, "he is...right."

"Then why are you here?" I asked.

"Because...there is nowhere else."

I looked back to the others, then to Guff, then around the entranceway of the house. I considered a solution. I heard the whipping of the turbine outside.

"Under the house is a cavity where cables from the fan lead to batteries," I said. "It is always dark. Would that suffice?

"It would."

"Then go there. Is Lows your proper name or do you prefer something else."

Lows lowered his head to close in on mine. I stepped back. "If you will...permit it. I would like...to be called...Leon."

Leon, I thought. What a bizarre and unexpected answer.

"Welcome Leon," I said. The figure turned away. He floated around the house and out of view on legs that moved like a stop-motion character.

"I fear this will come back to us," Guff said. He broke away and pounded his feet like a pouting child back into the living room.

*

I rocked slowly on the bench swing on the terrace. Every time I swung back, I could see the edge of the cove. The night was clear and illuminated. The introduction of Lows-Leon brought sobriety back to me.

"Once again," she said, "you have my admiration."

She never startled me and I allowed her to share the vacant seat beside me.

"Thank you Inari," I said.

"You may be tested like this again," she said.

"We'll deal with it. It's more than the house, we've learned. They can take the rocks, the fields, the few trees if they must." Even under the moonlight, I could see the fields of permanently blossomed purple flowers that encircled the house. It marked the border of everything that meant anything to me.

"Irani," I started, "Guff couldn't answer this, but I wanted to ask you. Skye...did you know her?"

"Of her, yes," she answered.

"She's a selkie, like the Celtic myth."

"Correct."

"What do you know?"

Inari looked out over the darkness and took in a lungful of moist air. "The half-breeds are few," she said. "There were three seals, four wolfwomen, six swan maidens--well, swans, cranes, doves and geese--two finfolk, a tennin, a ravenhaired, a lionlady, a manatee mistress, and a half dozen others which were never discovered. Each had their own rules to obey, without disobedience. Like them all, they were bound to a place. If uprooted, they wandered for centuries before bonding again. I had thought they had vanished."

"Tell me everything," I muttered.

She finally turned me and offered a smile from only one corner of her mouth. "As said, she could be one of three. Most of them require you hide their coat, for if found, they would immediately leave. If taken, she would be young and loyal, with a sadness you must tolerate. If your burn the coat, she becomes mortal and loses her bond with the sea. I believe that happened to the Irish one. Roonah of Aran, I think was her name was. Farosee of Kalsoy swam up north. She was bound to human form for one day every seven years, away from her husband."

"Husband?"

"The only selkie male. He had a story. As she was constrained, Farosee would assume human form once every seven years. She could return to the sea at any time but could only return to land seven years later. She had no love for the land. I only know of her being forced to wife once."

"And Skye?

"I am sure she spoke no lies. You sit here waiting, ten years in her case. Same bound as Farosee, one day she must go ashore. Most else is the same as her Irish sister, except Skye is...softer. She pains for her losses."

"She married before?"

"Long before your grandfather was in diapers. He never hid her coat. Could choose to return and she refused. But he was taken to sea and trapped in a storm. She took to seal and saved him...and that was the end of it."

I was leaning closer, resting my elbows on my knees. "The end?" I asked.

"She can become a woman for a man. However, if they are bonded and she changes back, she can never return to him as his wife. They had no children. Like the others, after ten years, she must make a choice. Burn the coat and become mortal or take the sea and never return."

I leaned back and swallowed what Inari said. I rubbed my hands on my legs. I knew there was no exception, no loophole to exploit. That was her convention and it could never change. Inari placed her hand over mine.

"I'm sorry, my friend," she said. "That's the cost. The more lovely they are--the more beautiful the soul--the more punishing the rules they are forced to follow. The monsters have so few."

"I wonder how many are left out there, surviving."

"Less than you hope. Some died by the hands of men. Some by the hands of us, though not as often. Some starved in darkness. So many fell to the appetites of those who hunt us." For the first time, I felt a flutter in Inari's voice.

"Do you fear it?" I asked her. I never thought them capable of it. It was such a normal response, one I never expected her kind to have. "Can you?"

"Do you believe in an afterlife?" she asked in return. I knew she wasn't changing topics.

I rolled the answer over in my mind a few times before speaking. "Would you consider it ironic if I said I was agnostic?" She didn't answer. "I was raised to keep an open mind, but the idea was never forced on me. Part of me wants there to be one. I mean the appeal of an immortal soul. Who'd want to blink into nothing? To be whole and aware, to amount to something and then suddenly to be zero. Honestly, it terrifies me. Guff

claims all of this is through the will of noegic, our will to make it happen. If
we explain away an afterlife, would it go away as well?" She didn't answer
that one either. Her kind idolized their elders for their age and uniqueness.
Beyond that, no others were segregated and promoted into a position of
worship. There were no priests or chiefs. No one was elevated to
godhood, despite mankind's insistence on doing so. "And what of you?" I
asked.

"Those gifted with immortality are denied a second chance for it," she
answered. "There is no place fated for us after we fade. If you believe
there is none destined for you, then we would be cursed to the same fate."

I let the sound of an especially loud wave crashing against the rocks
distract me from the current topic. One aspect of Irani that distinguished
her from the others was her awareness of a world that she knew didn't
make any sense. Her age had offered her a fragment of acceptable
humanity. Miran, Izee, and all the others weren't aware of their many
limitations. Guff knew and was one of the few exceptions, but he
embraced his convention. Inari wished for more. She wished she could
write her life the way she wanted, to erase her limitations and turn into
someone else. If Inari couldn't after so many years, then Skye never would
in my lifetime.

Ten years.

"You think she'll return?" I asked.

"As said, the more beautiful the soul…and hers is one the brightest. I
fear you may not encounter the best of us, but we are all that remains."

"Ten years," I repeated.

Inari finally offered a smile. "No worries," she said. "If she doesn't take you upon seeing this, she is mad. Any of us would burn our coat for you."

*

I could swear I was starting to lose my hair in the back. My dad had a full head. Before she passed, my mother showed me a photo of the cue ball that was my grandfather on her side. After that, I knew I was screwed. Six years to go and I was surely fated to have a huge bald patch by the end of it. I had also put on a few pounds. Not too much, just enough to form a crease that bisected my navel when I sat down.

I began writing what I knew. I doubted it would ever see publication or be read by anyone outside the house. I started with the selkies, first with Eilean of Skye, then to Roonah of Aran and Farosee of Kalsoy. I wrote about McGuffin the Encourager and Percival of Peripheral People. Pixis of Fruitful Soil, Kaareen of Unusual Spices, Izee the Curious, Miran is Playful, Geraz the Wolf, and Leon/Lows of Lakeside. If I could add weight to my writing, then perhaps someone, somewhere would believe in it enough to create another refuge.

I had a TV but rarely bothered. Every time I attempted to watch, high definition video greeted me displaying in perfect clarity the new manners in which people destroyed what others created. The talking heads offered their reasons. Oddly enough, when concerned about thinking up new rhymes for Miran, purchasing grains and soy-based milk for Guff, and ensuring the lights in the living room never illuminated its south-west corner, the volume of the problems of the outside world was always turned down.

"The door's knocking, William," Guff announced loudly.

Who would it be this time, I wondered. I had expected more traditional fairies and dwarfs by this point. Miran had been the only one with wings. I was still hoping to save a leprechaun or the last living unicorn. What joy that would be. I knew there was still an equal chance of being forced to offer salvation to a troll or chimera. I half-expected every time I opened the door to be instantly turned to stone by a gorgon. This was not a rational fear for an adult man to have in the 21st century.

Inari was temptation enough. This was ridiculous. As I opened the door, I noticed the new arrival suspended a foot off the porch, treading invisible water. Her blonde hair floated unrestrained. She had the smile and eyes of the Cheshire cat, the latter twinkling in the setting sun. A single piece of white linen began over her shoulder and draped around her several times, wrapping her arms and waist but leaving her legs exposed below the knee. Loose fabric drifted like her hair. She leaned forward to the edge of the doorframe and tipped her head to the side, studying the details of my face. She looked like she was at the sunset of her teens, which I knew was a lie.

"You have got to be kidding me," I muttered to myself.

"Is this salvation?" she said with a pronounced perk.

I shook my head and turned away. Just what I needed, an actual nymph. Why couldn't I have a brownie or a boggle? Even a goblin wouldn't be the source of as much frustration.

"Guff," I shouted, "handle this please."

Guff leaned out from the kitchen to stare down the hallway. His brow ridges sunk deep as his eyes widened. He leapt gracefully over the counter and walked briskly to the entrance. "GLADLY," he shouted. As we passed, I could tell he was pleased. "Hello, my lovely nymph," he addressed her, "and how shall we address you?"

"*Elisa the Riverblessed,*" she answered.

"Wonderful and beautiful. Elisa, would you please come this way?" She swam into the entrance and offered her hand, which he kissed. "And how did you find us?" Guff asked.

"It was difficult once I arrived on the island," Elisa answered, "My sight is limited over soil. A pleasant bus driver pointed the way."

I stopped and pirouetted. "Bus?" I snapped. "You said...bus?"

Guff turned to me. "You didn't think we all flew, did you?"

"A bus, though?" As I said it, I immediately knew whom. "A bus..." I whispered.

"Yes," Elisa said, oblivious, "even led me to the house."

I pulled my hands behind my back and hooked my thumbs as I moved around her to the door. I looped around the house and saw the still idling bus by the distant road.

"Have I wronged somehow," Elisa asked Guff.

"Not at all, my sweet. Please follow; there are questions you will need to answer."

I burst from the purple blossoms and ran faster than I had run in years to intercept the bus before it drove off.

"Billy!" I shouted as I waved. The door opened and there he was, still as always.

"My namesake, how you lad?" Billy asked.

I paused to catch my breath. "Okay. I'm okay. It's been too long. So, is this a regular stop on your route?"

"Only for special customers."

I took in a deep breath as I let my heart calm down. Finally settled, I asked him, "Are you human?"

"Of course," he scoffed. "If I wasn't, I wouldn't be able to drive the bus. As human as my father."

I remembered our past conversations, the mythology I had read. "So your mother," I said, "the daughter of Fand."

Billy's eyes lit up. "How did you know?"

"Your lighter. The name on the side."

"Ah…of course. Alas, most of the stories about her were wrong."

"You're a bridge," I stated. He smiled. "That explains a lot. I always thought you believed in my story a bit too readily."

"That had nothing to do with it."

"Well, if you have any other strange passengers, they're all welcome here."

Billy leaned from the bus and looked south in the direction of Portree. "If only humanity had such a refuge," he said.

I followed his eyes but wasn't sure what he was looking at. "I stopped watching television sometime ago," I said.

"I wouldn't bother checking. Nothing good to see…too much news."

"As you said, this may be the last patch of unspoiled land."

"Yes, but I was hoping I was wrong. How much more room do you have? I can see more coming."

"Depending on their size, I should do fine. If I had known what was to come, I'd have built a hotel."

"I think the locals would have found that suspicious." Billy grabbed the handle for the door. "I wish you well, William. I pass this road every day like a clock. If you don't see me, assume the worst. G'day, my boy."

He closed the door and drove off. I watched the bus as it vanished over the distant hill.

*

Guff had performed his agreed duty. He checked the books I had acquired, asked Inari if there was anything the texts had missed. He asked Elisa direct questions about her past and her convention. We all insisted on such formalities to prevent misunderstandings and to ensure a pleasant stay. I was more adamant after it took four days of Miran stabbing me before we figured out why.

Elisa was a bright sunshine in the darkest of days. She was a playful spirit that could never be captured by any mortal. The more forceful the restraints, the easier it was for her to escape. Few men had tried, for she could drown a victim with a kiss by turning to water and snaking down their throat. She had done so at least twice but ensured the acts were in self-defense and not predatory. We had to believe her on that. Her convention had allowed her to survive with few stories. She had never married though Guff believed she was nearly as old as Inari.

"Pixis minds the garden in the front," I said after I finally formalized my introduction. I pointed to the door facing the cove. "I mean that front, not," I pointed to the door facing the road, "that front."

It was late and Guff was tending to Geraz's water. I had always counted the kitchen as my throne room and I toured it for the floating Elisa.

"I bring in food from town which we can't grow here," I said. "Kaareen cooks what I can't. He has the Midas touch. Without the curse, that is."

"How pleasant," Elisa answered, still smiling. She was lying flat in the air on an ethereal mattress. The ends of her toga drifting to brush the wood floor. I was trying to keep a comfortable distance, which Elisa kept invading. I opened the dishwasher and began unloading.

"And you?" I asked, "What can you offer?" Guff had already asked this but I wanted to hear it from her.

"We are close enough to water," she answered. "I can bring rain."

I nodded. "That's good. Anything else I should know?"

She rolled on her back and arched her head to look at me inverted. "Anything else you would like?" she teased.

I tried to avoid eye contact as she inched closer. "I'm sure that's fine," I said.

"You are Weaver, are you not?"

"I am."

"Then I love you."

A glass in hand tumbled to the stone counter and broke. I looked down at the cliché and chuckled. I swept the shards into the sink and brushed the particles from my hand. If my arrivals had begun with her, I might have responded differently. All these months with Inari had tempered my reaction. Back then, I would have been shocked or annoyed or tempted. When I finally turned to Elisa, she was leaning closer. I stumbled back a step.

"Oh no…no no no no," I stuttered out, holding up my hands. "Let's put a stop to that right now."

"Is something wrong?" She stopped smiling.

"No, nothing," I answered as I avoided her and approached the opposite counter. I opened the utensil drawer and began reorganizing them.

When I turned to see her, her eyes had shrunk and her smile had withered to pouting pucker. Her hair color had shifted to a deep red. If I didn't know better, I would say she was getting older.

"Don't tell me you're one of those that turns into a monster if rejected," I said.

"But you cannot reject me," she sulked.

"Yes," I answered. I worked my way around her again, this time moving away from being pinned by counters in the kitchen. I entered the open area of the dining area. "I am sure I can. I won't have...whatever the hell it is you're doing in this house. I appreciate it, though."

"But you are Weaver," she pleaded, "and this is the house."

"Very true...but my heart is claimed by another. Ask around, you'll hear it from many."

"And she is here?" Elisa went vertical and held out her hands like she had been crucified.

"Not yet," I answered. I glanced at the calendar as if I didn't know. "Five more years...and counting...slowly."

Elisa drifted back and sat on the counter. She was no longer sulking but still wasn't smiling. "My apologies," she said. "My type knows where we bond and to who. But it is not you."

I took this as a good sign and took a step towards her. "Good," I said. I wasn't sure if I meant it. "Good," I repeated to reassure myself.

"I am mistaken," she added. "Misunderstanding."

"Of course." I left her there and began walking from the room. I felt she needed privacy.

"It is your son whom I will marry," she said to my back.

I stopped short of the stairs but didn't turn around. I let that thought sit with me a moment before climbing.

*

By spring of the following year, we would welcome four more. Banya of Open Ocean, our only mermaid, moved between the house and the cove. I figured her type would have faded with the numerous legends, but somehow one had made it through.

After her was Puggin-Ragga Zuuba, an annoying squat that kept stealing my socks. He was one of the most inhuman creatures that resided in the house, shaped like a hairless dog walking on human legs. Pixis would be joined by another dawnling, Emanuel of Plentiful Nectar. They could have gotten along better if he spoke anything other than Norn.

In March, another elder finally appeared. Lazarus was a stone gargoyle that perched atop my house and boasted such useful tricks as preventing birds from defecating on the roof and ensuring the house would never attract lightning.

I never suspected seeing to the needs of faeries would ever become tedious. Five years since the house was built, and I had gotten used to it all. They were no longer a considerable draw on my finances. Pixis and Emanual maintained a garden, which grew far too much food given the amount of sunlight it received. Elisa might have been tied to water, but her specific convention bound her to move both water and the wind that followed it. As such, the turbine would never stop spinning. I was finding fewer reasons to go into town. Nearly every house resident pitched in to keep it presentable. I felt a routine setting in. I would wake up to a rhyme, have breakfast offered to me by the best cook in the world, and end the morning by taking a twenty-foot long wolf for a walk. Flowers were always in bloom. By my whim, I could command the weather around me. It was feeling normal. Going into Portree, that felt irregular. Talking to people and trying to interpret what they meant from what they said. I had to gauge someone's intent, read between the lines, and worry about insulting some unknown ideology.

I spent the days fixing the roof or writing and painting when I felt inspired. I didn't need to mow the lawn or water the plants. The only skill I had been forced to pick up was sewing. On my last foray to Portree, I had picked up enough to sustain me for the entire winter.

It was then, on the cue that my life had found some sense of normality, my nemesis arrived.

NINE

"Guff, who is that?" I asked, looking through the rear window. Across the ever-blooming flowers was a figure pacing at the outskirts of the property.

Guff bent his neck to look up. "Next house you build," he said, "lower the windows."

I pulled an unused chair over to the glass. "Sorry," I said.

I could tell from this distance that the figure was at least six feet tall. He was wrapped in a black canvas duster topped with a matching ten-gallon hat. He walked with the help of a wrought iron cane, which sank deep into the ground. Neither Guff nor I could see the figure's face as it marched just beyond the flowers.

"Don't go to him," Guff said.

"Is he one you know?" I asked.

"No...and that means it is wrong."

"We've had those you don't know before. It could just be a person or another elder." I unlocked the door. A few of the other fae approached cautiously. They all saw the figure. A few stepped back. Miran flew away to hide.

"I warn you now, lad," Guff said, "this is not a greeting you will remember fondly."

"Warning heeded," I said as I left the house.

I shouldn't have been afraid but every step I took felt like I was stalking behind the devil himself. He wasn't six feet; he was seven. He was gaunt with liver spots on his exposed hands. I gave him a wide berth as I walked around to greet him.

"Excuse me," I said as genially as I could, "not seen your likes around here."

"I am necessary," he responded in a deep, raspy tone. "I have been brought here for salvation."

"And what is your convention?" I asked, growing suspicious. "Or do you have one?"

"I do not."

He had tanned leather skin that was peppered with craters. Dark muttonchops were trimmed to a sharp straight line connecting his ears to the corners of his mouth. His teeth looked yellow and eroded. The cane in his hand was sinking into the soil from its own weight. To me, he resembled the silent thug that hung behind the corrupt marshal in every western film. This one might have started the trend.

"But you do know this place," I said.

"I know it because you know it," he answered. I noticed that even though his mouth appeared normal. The hair of his muttonchops covered a seam that allowed a much larger opening if needed.

I smirked and nodded. "I figured you would arrive eventually," I said, "but I expected something a bit more…substantial." For some reason, I wasn't as afraid as when I had approached. I held up my hands, "No offense." I paused and corrected myself. "Actually I don't care if I offend so take it as you like."

"All of this," he said as he waved a withered hand to the property, "all of this built, all this spent...to sustain a delusion. Books will be written about you."

"Perhaps they will or perhaps they won't." I took a step back. I glanced at the house and saw nearly every resident cramming a head through the open door and nearby windows. The figure placed both hands on his iron cane, pushing it deeper. "Like all the other stories I have been reading of late," I continued, "I am sure they'll get most of the details wrong."

"Those stories are wrong because you wish them to be," he answered. "It would be too convenient for them to match. Yet so many other events appear convenient for your sake, William Weaver."

Knowing my name stopped shocking me five years ago. "I assume that would be my cue to say 'you have me at a disadvantage, sir'...except we both know who you are, don't we? Does your kind have names? You ever bother? Should I just call you demon?" I nudged my chin to the house. "They call you that, but to me, it means something wholly different." I slowly orbited the figure. "You don't have a name, do you?" I asked. "Should I make something up--"

"Your friend is from Scotland," the demon answered. "Father was born in England, allowing you dual citizenship. You paint a dream and scour the land until you happen to stumble into it."

"How about Dave?" I interjected. "Dave the Demon. Hmm, sounds too formal. Something disarming. How about Sheldon? Can we try Sheldon?"

"Did you check your head?" he asked.

I stopped mocking and looked confused. "My head?"

"You hit your head on a rock when you fell down that cove. Everything started then. You didn't bother to check or you didn't care."

I brought my hand to my forehead to check for a scar. I ran my fingers through my hair.

"First of all," I said, "I didn't hit my head. I fell but I didn't strike the rock."

"You don't remember hitting the rock," he countered. "Did you really think you would find a place matching your paintings? How many books have done the same? I know you have read at least one. There was an episode of Star Trek that did the same." Seriously, Star Trek? "It's not even an original concept. To follow a painting and find the girl of your dreams. And this place doesn't really match. You only made it so. Probably modified your paintings to believe your own delusion."

The demon smiled and I could see the seams along his sideburns begin to crease and pucker, wanting to open.

"If you were some fire-licking monstrosity from the abyss," I said, "I might actually be frightened of you."

"Best I could do given your neurosis," he answered.

"My neurosis? What does my mental state have to do with the house?"

He stepped forward and I found myself withdrawing. My hand brushed over a purple blossom. "I am not here for the house," he said. "I am from you...for you."

I smiled and nodded. It would have been too easy to disregard him if he was an acid-dripping beast that fed upon the souls of fairies. I was impressed at his talent for manipulation. I knew I was on the property and he stood just inches outside of it.

"Well, I appreciate the affection...but I prefer to see other people." He didn't laugh. I thought it was funny. "I get it," I continued. "Make me believe I am losing my mind, that I've got dementia. Then the house becomes normal and you walk in and kill everyone."

"How can I kill what does not exist? I am not here for the murder of innocents. I am here to save you."

"And why would you care for my sanity?" I asked.

"Because, like them, I am part of you...except I am the lingering fragment trying to repair the damage, to pull you from chaos before being lost."

"So, the symbolic gesture would be to allow you, my sanity, to destroy my delusions and empty the house, therefore recovering my common sense and saving my soul?"

"You could just walk away, see a doctor, take medication, have a scan to see if your brain suffered damage in the fall. In the end, you will rejoin society. You will be productive, fruitful. Eventually find love, given time."

"I found it, thank you," I said.

The demon laughed, pulling apart the seam in his face and opening his jaw. He had no more teeth outside of his normal mouth. "Separated but confident of her return," he mocked. "You encounter nymph and siren, falling at your feet in worship. You could bed any number, yet you reject them. Nothing like events in your real life."

"Or it's just a coincidence."

"Excuses...you make them already. Given time, you will make others. See the logic behind my argument. Your father is dead, William."

"That was not a delusion," I snapped.

"Very true."

"And I am just leading my father's example. You have to do what you want to do."

"Your father was a great man," the demon said. "But his eyes were open. He travelled while you remain still. He sought adventure where you conveniently have it brought to you. What is the most plausible explanation?"

I laughed and took a step forward, the perimeter of flowers separating us. "Ahh...Nice try," I said. "Have to rationalize it, don't you? You are asking me to explain my side, to offer a counterargument. Even if I offer you one, that's ammunition you could use to instill doubt. You are trying to get me to use logic to explain my side. But there is no explanation. It's just how it is." I spoke up as I knew they could hear me. "Those I protect are too important for me to try to defend them with arguments and civilized discourse. I also know why I was warned about coming out...why you don't threaten me. You want to talk to me. You know the longer we discuss this, the more reasonable you think you will sound."

"Every word chips away at the wall you have built around the truth," he said.

I looked around the expanse of the house and surrounding property. "I can see quite the distance you have to patrol. I could build a small village in this space."

"The more people you create, the more doubt will be raised."

"Well, I'm not David Koresh. You want a chair? Umbrella? No wait, I don't suppose you do--"

"I am the vanguard of industry," the demon snapped as he stepped to the very edge of flowers, "the forerunner of intelligence. My steps mark the frontier of reason. We have explained the universe, peered into the smallest scale and the widest scope. Those that follow live in the shelter of reality, a cosmos for the taking. Nothing is sacred or unexplained. This is how it should be, William."

"You think I don't know that!" I shouted back but was not angry. "You think I want us to stop building or expanding or learning. We should never stop...but I also don't believe we should give up the possibility of the impossible. There will always be room for fantasy."

"And death?" the demon asked. "When we finally understand why and how, people will no longer fear the end. As long as you maintain vigilance, your kind will still die. Like your father. Wouldn't you prefer to let their world pass? Lock them in the realm of dreams. You could still live to a time to finally deny death itself. The alternative...remain here, holding back everyone else, letting them die, hoping there is an afterlife waiting, one that you know may not exist. Would you follow your father to that end?"

"My father also said to enjoy life, regardless of the risk. My father died young...but he died happily. There's nothing I want out there." I turned and made my way back the house. The demon didn't follow.

"Isn't that selfish?" he asked.

"Look at my ward! Look at whom I protect. I don't care if my people never know of it." I pointed to the house. "They do...and that's all that matters."

I reached the house and Guff jumped out from the shelter. "Yeah, and you know what," he shouted, "I second everything he said." The squat made an obscenity with his hand. "Plus a finger up your butt!"

"Guff!" I shouted.

"Not helping?" Guff asked.

"Go back!" shouted Elisa to the demon. Wrinkles sunk into her face as she said it. They would fade when her mood improved.

"I never will as long as William carries even the smallest fragment of doubt," the demon answered.

"He doesn't doubt," Guff snapped.

"William is salvation," Miran squeaked. "He built us this mansion!

"*Sie sind minderwertig*," shouted Izee.

"No more will arrive," the demon said. "I will ensure that. If any attempt to leave, they will not return."

From around the garage, Geraz the wolf leapt out. The massive animal circled around the demon, inching closer with each orbit. It glared its teeth and growled loudly.

"Geraz...back," I ordered. Geraz ignored me and opened its jaw to bare its teeth to its opponent. "Come here!" I shouted again.

The wolf brought up its back and tightened its legs. It wound its strength for a great leap.

"Geraz!!" I screamed.

The demon opened its hand and Geraz froze inches from its prey. The seam along the demon's mouth opened and the huge maw expanded larger than its head. Geraz lost all bravery and I could tell he was instantly terrified. The fae behind me were frozen. I didn't know what to do. Geraz was paralyzed.

There was no blood as the wolf shredded apart. His fur and skin flayed like unpeeling an orange. There was nothing inside save for a puff of orange smoke. It started to drift away but was caught by the vortex churned up by the demon's mouth. The demon devoured every wisp and closed its jaw. The fallen tatters of Geraz drifted with the breeze as if they were tissue paper.

The fae behind me screamed. I turned quickly to face them.

"Everyone inside, now!" I snapped.

They did so and I followed them. I slammed the door and locked both bolts. Miran and Izee were still staring through the window. Inari was holding a despondent Elisa. Guff was searching the living room, hoping to stumble upon some previously unseen weapon.

"We knew this was going to eventually happen," I said. "A beast formed between the two worlds."

"Geraz," Elisa whimpered.

"The courageous fool," snapped Guff. "Wrong time for bravado."

"No one goes beyond the purple blossoms," I said, arms crossed. "I don't think I need to repeat that."

"That fate awaits us all," Elisa cried.

"No, it won't," I replied firmly.

"And what of you?" Percival said from the corner, "What if you die?"

"Don't worry about that," I said.

"Centuries free," Elisa cried, "now only decades, locked in a house. Some salvation—"

"Stop it," Guff snapped. "William gave up everything for this."

"It was not like we were going to leave anyway," Inari whispered, as she caressed Elise's hair.

I walked back to a window and parted the drapes to see the figure slowly pacing outside the flowers between the house and the road. "At least we know where the border lies," I said. "Actually bigger than I thought."

"What now?" Inari asked.

"Continue as before," I replied. "We have space; let's make the most of it."

"Expand the garden," shouted Pixis.

I pointed to her. "Good idea."

"A shed," Percival volunteered.

"Yes."

"Greenhouse," Elisa said, adding the beginnings of a new smile. I shifted my finger pointing to her.

"Now that is brilliant."

"A bank vault," added Guff.

I moved my finger to Guff but pulled back when I realized what he suggested. "That we can do without," I said. "Make a list."

"Maybe a dock, by the water?" Marik offered.

"In contrast to a dock on dry land?" Guff mocked.

A few fae snickered but my smile sunk to a grimace when it occurred to me.

"Wait…can he swim?" I asked, looking at Inari. If anyone knew, it would have been her."

"I do not know," she answered.

I ran out of the front door, towards the cliffs. Only Miran was fast enough to pursue. Lazarus leapt from his perch and followed to the edge.

I dropped from the edge and skidded down to the cove. I had done it so often I never stumbled.

"Banya!" I shouted. "Banya of Open Ocean!"

The topless mermaid poked from the cold ocean. She didn't dip or rise with the waves. She remained perfectly still as if standing on a pedestal in the water.

"You seldom call me, William," she answered.

"Are you safe?"

"We are never safe. No one ever is. Ignorance is paradise. Insight…is enlightenment."

"And where do you stand on that?" I asked.

"We have an antagonist."

"In the literary sense of the word," I said, playing off her response. "Can he reach you?"

Banya looked up to the top of the cove, then back to me. Her smile harkened to a time when she pulled ships into the shallows to wreck.

"You claimed the water when she touched you," she answered. "I will be as safe as she. I will ensure her passage when the time comes."

*

It was less than a week later when Miran noticed the next arrival. She flew behind me and stuck me in the neck with her minuscule dagger.

"OW, Miran!" I shouted. I held my neck and could feel the dripping blood. I grabbed a tissue and held it in place. "You didn't even say anything that time!"

"Another fairy!" she shouted, "Just around that tree!" That got the attention of the others.

"Well, let's see," I answered. Rhyming had been a reflex. I no longer gave it any thought.

We noticed only a small shape from this distance. It could have been a bird but Miran was adamant. It was beside a family of spruce trees sitting by the road. Miran must have possessed some talent to spotting her own kind we were unaware of.

"It won't make it through," Guff said. "If the demon senses there's one out there, he'll devour it."

"William must save her," ordered Miran. Good to know she was offering solutions.

"I will," I answered, "that you can be sure."

"But how?" Guff asked.

I kept an eye on the demon as he sauntered around the outskirts of the property. It finally dawned on me and I straightened my back.

"Why am I afraid? He can't harm me. That invalidates every argument he's been trying to make. I walked to the coat rack and retrieved my worn but priceless heavy wool and polyester black long coat. "I'm just going to walk right past him." I donned the jacket and held it tight like it was chainmail. "I'll leave for Portree, circle to the road. Find some way to get past."

Miran nodded and said nothing. Guff stepped in front of me as I made for the door.

"But he can read your mind," he interjected. "He'll know. Every deceit, every trick."

That was true. It would read my intent to seek out the creature hiding in the forest. Why it didn't know already was anybody's guess. Perhaps the walls of the house were a shield protecting me as well——the demon not knowing anything until I walked out to greet it. I stepped back and looked to the others, hoping they would have a solution.

"I am not known for emptying my mind," I replied. They said nothing. Miran was still expecting me to solve it on my own. To her, my life was dependant on rescuing this one creature and that was all that mattered. I turned back to Guff. "Guff, you've been brewing, correct?" I asked.

"Correct," he answered.

*

It was peppered vodka, of all the drinks for Guff to make in his spare time. The spiced flavor came from Kareen. I was only six shots in when I started to mumble. Guff was pounding down equal numbers beside me but showed no signs of inebriation. I glanced at him and the others around me.

"You guys are so small, you know that?" I slurred. Guff smiled as Elisa poured another drink. "Why are you drinking?" I finally asked the squat.

"You drink, I drink," Guff answered. "I barely need an excuse as it is."

"You can get drunk?" I asked, knocking back another.

"Not horizontal drunk, just slightly diagonal."

Elisa poured another. I wasn't sure at what point my mind would be so chaotic that the demon wouldn't be able to read it. I wasn't even sure if it would even work. As Elisa topped the glass, I placed my hand on hers.

"You know, Elisa. You…are an extremely attractive nymph, you know that?" I was sure it didn't come out that articulate.

"Yes, William," she answered, "I'm supposed to be that way. Now behave. I'm promised to another as you are bound to another."

I released her hand and leaned back.

"I know, I know." I got distracted by a fluttering fairy that buzzed around my head. If I wasn't drunk, I could have mistaken it for an illusion. "I'm just saying I don't want you to think I rejected you because I thought you were ugly in any way. Or that you looked weird with that smile or those eyes. Or that I was still kinda smitten with Inari—who I'm also not interested in, just wanted to say."

Elisa smiled. She looked as young as the day I first met her. After Geraz died, she had taken on lines and spots that brought her into her fifties. It took some time for her to recover from that.

"I know," she replied.

"But I wanted to say it," I persisted, like an idiot. "You are an extremely…beautiful and when I have my…wait…only son? One kid or will I have many?"

"I don't see the future, my sweet. It may even be a grandson. I just know he will be here and he will be named William."

"Ahhh," I burped. "Irregardless—"

"That is not a word," Guff interjected. He was getting frustrated at my continued chatting.

"Yes it is."

"Now I know you are drunk, William. Irregardless is not a word."

"Fine," I snapped, rolling my head back to Elisa, "REGARDLESS, I wanted to clear the…" I drifted away and looked back to Guff. "What was I going to do?"

Irani answered, "Go the forest beyond the house and bring back the fairy."

I nodded. "Right…right."

The door opened and I staggered out of the house. I took my time and placed my steps carefully. I wasn't sure why I was doing this. I was sure it would come back to me in a few minutes. I wobbled down the path back to the road. As I reached the periphery of purple blossoms, I noticed the demon leaning on his iron cane. I meandered closer.

"Hey DOD," I shouted. The creature grimaced in my direction. "That's what your name will be. I just decided. DOD. You like it?" It didn't answer. "It stands for Demon of Doubt. I think it fits."

I snaked around him as he answered. "You risk walking from your prison?"

"Can't hurt me," I taunted, "now or ever." I turned to walk down the road. I shuffled about as I lost balance

"Please be my guest, then," DOD answered. "The more time you spend in town, the more you will realize what you are missing, the life you abandoned."

"Not a good argument since the nearest town has hardly changed in two hundred years. T-T-Y-L." I continued to wander towards Portree. I looked back and saw DOD continue his patrol around the house. After he vanished around the front, I diverted quickly back up to the patch of spruce trees. DOD's course would take him to the edge of the rocks, as my property included the cove and the beach. He would then turn around and circle back, repeating a horseshoe route to the other side.

I couldn't remember exactly what I was supposed to do, something about finding a fairy stuck in a tree. It was such a ludicrous thought; it had to have been the right one. I clumsily pushed through the bushes.

"Hey little buddy," I whispered. "I know you're here." I pushed through the branches, unsure what I was going to find. It was not so much a forest, with only a half dozen trees surrounding me. I didn't see the stump and I found myself stumbling into the soft dirt, barely missing a large rock. I pulled my chin from the divot it made in the soil and saw him staring back.

He was just under a foot tall and wore pristine gilded mail with a matching golden helm. He covered his linked rings with the glossiest set of plates I had ever seen. He had a splash of blue paint across his cuirass. From gauntlets to pauldrons, his arms were a fortress. The blade on his back was an intimidating four inches long, four times that of Miran's. I hoped this one wouldn't stab me. Unfortunately, I was drunk, and I found the sight extremely humorous.

"You're a brownie!" I squealed.

"I'm a *fee*, monsieur," he spat back. The accent was as thick as cold oil.

"Oh god," I laughed, almost burping, "you're French. That's...adorable."

"And *vois, monsieur*, are drunk. How can you see me?"

"I run the house. You have a name?"

"*Chevalier* Philip Le Grand of 'de Order of Saint Michael," he proudly answered.

"*Chevalier*?" I asked. "Were you knighted or something?"

"King Louis 'de Eleventh was a personal friend of many years." His nose was actually upturned.

"Wasn't Louis insane?" I had read a lot in the past few years.

Philip's pomposity dropped off. "Dat was King Charles 'de Fourth," he answered.

"Oh right," I said, "Louis was the Spider King."

"Misunderstood. Oh de' pure soul punished for 'dis clarity of thought."

"Well," I said in an attempt to focus the conversation, "we should get going, little buddy." I looked back to see if DOD had emerged from the other side of the house. He was taking his time.

"I have demands, monsieur," he snapped.

I had little control over my neck muscles so my head bobbed and flopped about as I stood up.

"This is not a situation which permits negotiations, sir knight," I said, taking another glance at the house.

"I must have a pillow of silk," he barked. "There must be champagne and I will not abide raisins."

"That's a strange convention," I replied.

"Who said it was my convention?"

"I'll see about the silk," I said. I took a knee and opened my coat. "Now shall we?" I could hear the fabric ripping in my inside pocket as he fell into it. His various corners and edges dug into my side.

"By the way," I said before closing the coat, "I have a rat you'll absolutely love."

I waited over the hill until I was certain DOD had circled around the other side. I quickened my pace, shuffling my awkward feet. When I got close to the house, I noticed the shadow of the demon sticking from around the corner, but it wasn't moving. Something bothered me about that so I stopped.

"What's 'de problem, monsieur?" Philip asked.

"We have to watch for the demon," I replied.

"Demon? You have a sanctified sword, monsieur? To dispatch 'dis adversaire?"

I said slowly, "I must have left it with my plate mail."

I crept closer to the property. The shadow wasn't moving. I was still fifty feet from the purple blossoms when we noticed DOD walking back like he was waiting for me to make my approach.

"He's coming back," Philip whispered. "He knows. We'll never make it."

I walked faster. I wasn't sure if DOD would become violent, if he would physically force the fee from my protection. He didn't appear to notice us or was pretending not to. I didn't know if his power had reach. Could he teleport or extend his arms? Thirty feet from the property, we fell into a shadow cast by a large stone. It felt like falling into motor oil. The black clung onto me and pulled me under but it was neither wet nor suffocating. Under the surface, we could look up to the ground like a pane of glass. Despite the light from the opening, we were still bathed in shadow.

Neither Philip nor I moved. We heard the steps of the demon, the heavy thud of his wrought iron cane. I noticed the top of his cowboy hat drift by. One minute passed, then another. I kept my breath shallow. After what felt like a full commercial break, I felt the viscous ground push me back to the surface. The black peeled itself from my skin as I climbed back into sun. I stood and looked around for DOD. He had walked around the property again. I ensured Philip was unharmed. I began to walk to the flowers, but then stopped and turned back to the shadow.

"Thank you, Leon," I said.

TEN

Phillip was the last. It was possible there were no others out there. We could see DOD patrolling the perimeter but never saw him claim another soul. Lazarus had taken it upon himself to keep a vigilant eye. Pixis, Miran, and Emanuel slipped through flowers along the edge of the property, stealing looks to the outside world in hopes of spotting one of their own hidden amongst the grass and trees.

The garden grew. Wind was plentiful. I had little reason to leave, though I had been forced to do so on a few occasions, replacing shingles and what not.

Three weeks past my twenty-ninth birthday, there was a knock on the door. Every fae stood. They ran or flew if they could to the door. Guff blocked their path to the hallway. It had been so long since one had come.

"Wait, don't assume fantasy," he whispered, holding his index to his lips. "This could be a threat." He made room as I passed him.

"Err on the side of caution," I said.

Pixis squeaked quietly, "The demon's come right to the door."

"Nonsense you silly fae," Guff snapped. "It wouldn't knock if it could get this close. It would just come in. This could still be an outsider."

"Census taker?" Inari guessed. "Salesman?"

"Or worse," Guff answered, "Jehovah's Witness."

I made room and opened the speakeasy. I noticed the ordinary figure standing on the porch. I recognized him instantly. I closed the speakeasy and turned to the others.

"You all need to hide," I whispered. "Be quick and quiet about it. Stay out of sight."

"Who is it?" Guff answered while the others followed my instructions.

"No matter what, don't make a sound," I ordered. "Keep the others in line. I must deal with this myself."

"If he's a normal, don't let him convince you."

"Don't worry."

Guff shepherded the others to the upstairs rooms. Miran was the harder one to corral. Elisa finally floated up, snatched her by the wings, muffled her, and dragged the rebellious fairy into the bedroom. I hoped Lazarus would remain in stone like he did most hours of the day. I unlocked the door and welcomed my guest.

"Colin," I said, acting surprised.

"William," Colin answered. He aged well, having kept in shape with a physical discipline I obviously lacked in the intervening years. He still had his full head of strawberry hair.

"What the hell?" I replied. "What are you doing here?"

"I was visiting the homeland," he paused. I knew he was trying for a lie. We knew better so he stopped trying. "And yeah, I came to see you as well."

"Well, I guess I should invite you in." I opened the door wide to welcome him. He stepped in slowly like stalking into Tutankhamen's tomb.

He took off his shoes but kept his coat on. He said nothing until he entered the living room. He took a moment to take in the similarities.

"Holy crap," he said. "It's uncanny."

"Thank you."

"I mean it's exact…well." He waved to the corner of the living room. "I don't remember the fake fireplace." The place looked spotless. Guff had cleaned only minutes prior. Colin turned back to me. "Just you?"

"Just…yeah, just me."

"Nobody?"

"No."

"Ever?"

"Why?" I said with a laugh. I wondered what he knew. Did he hear voices? The walls and the door were quite thick. Perhaps he had been outside for several hours. Perhaps he had looked into the rooms, seen the truth, and was playing ignorant.

"Awful lot of space," he replied.

"Want coffee?" I asked. I didn't wait for an answer. I made my way around the kitchen counter. I tapped on the electric kettle. It already had water from a previous tea. I wasn't much for coffee but like so many things, I kept it around. I pulled two large black mugs from a cupboard. They both were engraved with the "Pi" symbol.

"What are you doing?" Colin finally asked after a minute of uncomfortable silence.

"Coffee," I joked as I spooned instant grounds into his mug. I then placed a bag of Orange Pekoe in mine.

"I mean here?" he said. "What did this accomplish?"

"You don't want to know."

"I'm here," he said plainly. I still wasn't sure if he had seen something he shouldn't have, or if he had heard me talking from outside. I wonder if the flowers perfectly encircling the estate concerned him. Did he wonder why there was a stone gargoyle atop the house? We never lied to each other so I knew starting now would disrespect him. Any explanation would make me appear crazy. At least the truth offered me a measure of self-respect.

"I'm running a refuge for outcast fairies," I said directly. The water was boiling. The light clicked off the kettle as I removed it from its stand. I poured the cups full and dropped in spoons. "Milk and sugar?"

"Black."

I offered him the cup while I poured hazelnut-flavored, dairy-free coffee whitener into mine. We shared a moment of sipping. I finally broke the silence.

"You took that well."

"I'm not sure I know you well enough to assume you were joking."

"You're going to tell me I'm insane regardless of what I say. If I told you I was living in a replication of my father's house in the middle of nowhere, squandering my inheritance, you would still claim me crazy. I might as well tell you the truth."

"Then I don't know you because I'm still not sure if you're joking or not. What of the woman? The dream?"

"She was one of them, *is* one of them. She's yet to arrive. Won't be long now. These past years, others have arrived, forced from their homes by industry and common sense."

"And they're here? Where would they be?" Colin asked.

"They kind of don't dig your jive, Colin," I joked. "I could ask. They could come out. It would change things, maybe to the house, definitely to you." I took another long sip. "You don't want to see them. You would get angry…at me."

The tea was still too hot, even with the whitener. Colin's coffee must have been scorching but he still forced it down his throat. He sat where Guff sat when he and I first met.

"What of yourself?" I asked. I wasn't avoiding the topic. "What have you been up to? You get your degree?"

Colin nodded. "Yes," he said. "I didn't abandon that."

"So what do you do?"

"I work for a company called Slipware—"

"Pottery?" I interrupted. Colin scowled like I had just punched a puppy.

"What? No."

"Just saying it's a pottery term, like two thousand years now—"

"It's a software company, networking management," Colin retorted.

"Do they network kilns?" I joked.

"If they had computers, yes. We were on the cover of Wired last year."

"Do you actually think I subscribe?"

"Well, I wasn't aware you'd forsaken all modern vices. Still got a TV, I see."

"I hardly ever use it. No time with all my errands. Taking care of the residents is practically a full-time job. No satellite anyway. You enjoy this job?"

Colin stopped the quick banter and took a breath. He had heard what I said and it reminded him of the topic he was trying best to ignore.

"Yes and the pay's phenomenal," he answered. "Three cars."

"And I imagine a sizable house to hold them."

"And a time share in the Algarve," Colin added with his head down.

"Then I guess you truly have achieved an acceptable measure of success. Glad we both made something of our lives. Got kids? A wife? Someone finally corral you into monogamy?"

"Dude," he said, "you need to stop this."

"I neither want to nor need to."

"You've completely lost it."

"Don't follow," I answered as I took my stool on the opposite side of the counter.

"You spent every dime to build a house in the middle of nowhere, exactly the same house you already owned. And I find you here, alone, talking to faeries."

"Would you prefer I lied?"

"Maybe," he answered. "I do want you to present them."

I shook my head. "You ask because you want to prove to me it's not real. If you were willing to believe, maybe I would. But I can't do it. You're noegic."

"I'm what?"

"Noegic...the opposite of magic." I tipped forward and leaned my hands on the counter. "This isn't some rhetoric of fairies dying if you don't believe in them. Clapping won't do shit. It's called the radiance of noegic. *Neosis*...the Greek word for *understanding*--that much I figured out on my own. If you explain something logically, you enforce logic. Logic? Magic? Get it? If you enforce one, the other fades. Noegic is the word they use."

Colin nodded. "Very," he started.

"Self-fulfilling," I answered for him.

"Yeah, kinda."

"If we all died out, they would prosper. They don't need us. Never did."

"So what is this?" Colin said. He pointed to the room with his half-full mug. "The entire universe was magic? We started to explain it, and it all made sense...retroactively?"

I genuinely laughed. "Funny, I said nearly exactly the same thing at the beginning."

"Are you listening to yourself? It makes no sense."

I gave him the point of a bent finger. "Exactly," I said.

"And you've been doing this for...ten years?"

I nodded. I looked out the nearest window, then to the fridge calendar.

"It's been ten years," I said. "Ten years. Interesting you arrive now. It's only five days away."

"What is?"

"Ten years exactly from when I first arrived."

"And how much do you have left, money I mean?"

"I'm doing ok," I answered. "House is good. You like the garden outside? The flowers?"

"What flowers?" Colin asked. He looked confused but I ignored it.

"Did you happen to see a man by the road?" I asked. "Kinda looks like a cowboy."

"No."

"Huh," I said to myself. "I wonder if he's behind this."

"What?"

It would make perfect sense. I never thought DOD was capable of it but it wouldn't surprise me. It was five days to ten years. The timing could hardly be coincidence. In the house, that reasoning would be enough but out there, everything had to have a reason. Someone encouraged Colin to leave at that point, to be here at this moment.

"You being here," I replied.

"I came because I wanted to see what happened. I tried to prepare myself for anything." Colin looked around the pristine house again, "but this? Shall I be blunt?"

I brought the tea to my lips. "And you haven't been so far—"

"I think you've had a psychological breakdown," Colin interjected. "I don't think you fully recovered from your father's death. You want there to be more. You want your life your way so you're making it up."

I took my time to swallow and cupped the warm mug in my hands. "Did you have any problem finding the place?" I asked.

"What does that have to do with anything?" Colin snapped.

"Just asking if you got lost getting here...at any point."

"No, I found it easy."

"Yeah, I know why."

"Excuse me?" Colin was getting angrier.

"Trying to instill doubt," I explained, "make me think I'm delusional. That this was all a waste of time."

Colin braced his elbows on the counter and held up his palms like he was a priest blessing the sacrament. "What I think," he paused, speaking slowly to ensure I heard him clearly, "you should do...is put the place for sale. Try to recoup some money for it. Come back with me. Let me get you some help. Get back into painting, get back your career." His voice was breaking from trying to act calm. Moments of fury were pushing through. "Salvage something. This is not going anywhere."

I wasn't sure what to say. I knew he was well intentioned.

"I appreciate your honesty," I replied. *"Se seo an fàth a bhi mi beò."* My accent and vernacular were perfect.

"What is that?" Colin asked.

"Gaelic. I've become quite fluent."

"So you actually think it's real." It sounded more like a statement. Colin hadn't taken in coffee since the "blunt" comment. I didn't blame him. It wasn't very good.

My conversations with Guff had hardened me to the philosophical concerns over what I was doing. I had read once in an article that there was actually a scientific probability that the entire human race was experiencing a shared delusion—a virtual reality of sorts.

"If it's tangible within my perception," I replied, "what does it matter if you can't perceive it? Does that make it less real?" I was trying to make an argument about the perception of human senses and its capacity to see only a very small portion of the observable universe. Colin was having nothing to do with it.

"Yes," he snapped. "A thousand people seeing a UFO doesn't change the fact it was a plane. All that crap I read about if you believe in something it will happen. People say that to make themselves feel better. To make them think they have some control over this world. That's the problem right now. Look outside; see what's going on around you. Half the planet thinks Morgan Freeman is going to swoop down in a white suit and save them and the other half is too scared to oppose the other. I thought you weren't religious?"

"I'm not," I countered. I understood his point. In his eyes, there has to be something measurable to believe it exists. Although I respected his point, I had issues with it. Even in science, there were experiments that altered their expected results when they were measured. "You're confusing knowing with faith. You also think by saying it makes no sense, by rejecting the normal world, that suddenly I'm a bible thumper. Well, perhaps everyone is wrong…have you thought of that?" I paused but continued before Colin could make an argument. "Perhaps fantasy and science is all about perception. You chose to explain things, like scientists, like priests. I'll still be here…holding the torch of chaos."

"But you won't prove it by bringing out one, just one fairy. One leprechaun—"

"I never got a leprechaun," I interrupted. "I'm very bummed about that."

"Anything…what do you got?"

"The problem is that you'll not believe it. You're not one that'll accept something that can't be explained. I could present every one and you'll walk away and discount it somehow. You'll find some explanation. Swamp gas or something."

"And you don't want me to," Colin assumed. He was right.

"No…I don't."

"Because you can't accept the fact that the last ten years was a waste."

"No," I snapped back, "because this house is more important than me."

"Your sanity is less important than an empty house?"

"I'm not insane," I said plainly. He wasn't getting me angry. I didn't want to start an argument. This was the longest conversation I've had with another human in ten years. Colin lifted his cup to sip. He squirmed as he swallowed. He put the mug back down and pushed it to me. I took the cup and dumped the cold coffee into the sink. I did the same with my tea.

"Okay, I didn't want to say this, but obviously I have no choice." Colin reached into his pocket and removed a folded legal paper. Microscopic text filled every inch. It was five pages of scientific jargon compressed into a single sheet.

"What's that?"

"Prussian blue," Colin answered.

"Prussian blue?" I was surprised by the remark.

"Before you make a stupid joke, I know what the color is and yes, the text is black."

"What about Prussian blue?"

"You used it. Still do?"

"It's in my collection."

"It was recalled." Colin pushed the paper across the counter. I caught before it fell. "I didn't know pigments were used in medicine. Apparently, it can treat heavy metal poison."

I had no scientific background. I also had no interest in focusing on the technical jargon of the paper, especially since I was sure Colin was going to translate it for me anyway.

"I'm sure you'll narrow this line of conversation into something direct."

"The art company listed in the recall purchased contaminated pigment from a chemical company whose primary export is for pharmaceutical clients."

I looked over and confirmed the company. I still ordered from them. I still had Prussian blue, still had the same bottle I hadn't finished in ten years. I took good care of my paints.

"Still waiting," I goaded.

"It was tainted with DMT," Colin snapped. I looked at the extremely long word associated with the recall.

"Dimeth—Dimethyl—Dimeth—" It was really long.

"Dimethyltryptamine," Colin said perfectly. He had practiced.

"And that is?"

"It's in the tryptamine family."

"Still with the big words. You know I don't have Wikipedia here."

"It's a hallucinogenic!" Colin shouted. "That direct enough for you?" I let the top half of the paper fall over its fold. I didn't need to see its facts. I wasn't stupid enough to read it.

"That's it?" I asked.

"You have nothing to say about it?"

"First of all, recalls like this are to protect that one idiot that eats paint. I had it on my fingers. I wasn't licking it."

"It can go through the skin."

"And you're saying all of this was from tainted paint? I'm a layman. I'm smart enough to know that's a stretch."

"I am saying you were contaminated ten years ago and the trauma of your father caused your brain to rewire. DMT can be produced by the body as well. I think you got this in your system and your body's been doing the rest."

"Psychedelics can't do this. Not a perpetual fabrication that doesn't deconstruct. You see, I can use big words too. And this is a pervasive truth with its own rules I didn't create. These individuals never change. They have language. They have emotions. They can stab you if you don't say the right thing. They affect reality."

"Your reality."

"That's the only one I know...and can ever truly know."

I threw the folded paper back onto the counter. Colin didn't accept it. He pressed his lips together and tried to bottle his frustration.

"I wish," he said. "I wish I'd never encouraged you to come here. It's my fault. I should've known something was wrong. Why did I encourage you? The painting was a symptom. I didn't see it."

He was adamant about my sanity. In his defense, he was right...in the symptoms, not his diagnosis. He was a computer engineer; what did he know? It would have been a sensible assumption that I had undergone some psychological trauma. I wanted badly to prove him wrong. Who would I walk out, Inari, Guff? They looked too normal. Leon would be to frightening. I could whistle for Pixis or Miran. If seen, Colin would immediately accuse me of spiking his coffee. He would offer a family of reasons why both he and I were seeing the same thing. DOD expected and wanted that.

"There was a moment you could you have made that leap," I said. "If you were that teenager I remembered, I probably would show you. But that's not you anymore."

"Ten years in the real world will do that to someone," Colin said. He grimaced. "It's called adulthood." If I didn't know any better, I would swear Colin regretted saying that, like a part of him envied me.

"It must be really bad out there," I assumed.

"Almost to the point that I would want to believe you...just so I could hide as well." Despite that ray of hope, I still knew Colin wouldn't be able to make that leap. One just can't break from some hardwired programming.

"But you can't," I replied. "You won't let yourself."

Colin brought his head up to stare directly at me. I didn't know what he was going to say if he was. He was as close to a blank slate as a stranger. I noticed, in that long moment of silence, a scar covered by his mop of hair. It wasn't an accident. Something had been removed or put in. He wore a wedding band but it was on the wrong finger. I didn't know if that signified anything.

"William," Colin started, then paused for a breath, "I won't come back."

"Yeah, I know," I answered.

"I'm not a tough love guy. If you won't help yourself, I won't bother with it."

"Yeah, I know. If you do decide to come back, I will show you. However, you have to come back knowing that your life will change. You have to open your mind...and right now, it's not. Regardless, it was good to see you again."

Colin didn't say much after that. He still had his coat on. He rolled off the stool and sauntered to the exit. I followed him out. We walked around the house to Colin's rental Ford Fiesta. I could see the silhouette of DOD at the edge of the property, standing beside the trail that connected the house to the road. He was near invisible, obviously keeping himself out of sight as part of the strategy. Convincing Colin would have gone far in my favor. DOD wouldn't have pulled the strings of an ordered society to convince Colin to come here if he doubted his resolve, another reason why I knew it wasn't wise to try to convince him.

"Well, I guess I should say enjoy what you got," Colin said as we shook hands, "though I'm not sure what you have."

"Thanks…and don't worry about it," I replied. "You did the best you could."

Colin opened the door, entered the car, and started the engine. He slowly made his way back down the road. I followed until the edge of the flowers and watched the car's lights vanish over the hill. DOD materialized from the shadow and approached me.

"Your friend was right," he growled.

"Was he?" I asked back.

"You're actually suffering from a toxin contamination. The house is empty. Every inhabitant in that building is a fabrication of your own delusion."

I turned from the road to walk to the house. "You should change your script. You've said pretty much the same thing for a year. You brought him."

DOD hooked my arm with his iron cane and gently turned me around. "How could I do that?" he asked.

"You found a way. It was good to have seen him…but I wished he could believe."

"You didn't give him a chance."

I freed myself from the cane. "I know him. He would never have accepted it." I walked away from DOD but took my time returning to the house. "Been good talking to you, DOD."

I was visibly unhappy as I opened the door. My human contact was growing more infrequent and I feared that conversation was the last of it. I closed the door and leaned against it. They were already emerging from their hiding places.

"Are you ok?" Guff asked, the first to approach. I didn't answer.

"We respected your wishes," Inari said. The others had gathered around. "We could have shown him."

I shook my head. I don't know why I so depressed. I hadn't thought about Colin for a long time. Perhaps I just didn't care to be reminded of the other world. Perhaps it was something else. How many people will DOD dangle before me before I start to believe them? There were few of those left. Fewer still that cared.

"I can't drag him into this," I said. "He's spent his entire life accepting what he sees. I can't destroy what he believes."

"Even though he just tried to do the same to you?" Guff said.

"But it was out of friendship. He's looking out for my best interests."

"You think he will come back?"

"No," I answered. I'll never see him again." My eyes desperately wanted to shed tears and holding them back was causing a significant headache.

"I am sorry," Inari said. A drop finally rolled down my left cheek. I wiped it off. It didn't help that everyone was still staring.

"The first time I've seen you sad," Elisa said, pouting like a twelve-year-old. "Don't let me see that again."

"You think DOD brought him?" Guff asked, trying to change the topic.

"It's likely," I answered.

Elisa swam around Inari and approached me. She drifted
Around my back and whispered in my ear.

"If you prefer," she said. "I could fog this land."

"Fog?"

"I could bring weather to conceal the house. It would only appear so
to those outside. Here, it would still be beautiful. But those who doubt
would never see it."

The beacon atop the house--the invisible fire that never burned—
could be seen regardless of time of weather. She wouldn't have offered it if
she felt it would shroud the house to them. It would protect us from further
introgressions by DOD's disciples of order. It would ensure that no human
would ever see the house again.

"Do it," I said.

ELEVEN

I was certain I had gained at least twenty pounds, perhaps thirty, in the past ten years. I was attempting to squeeze into the same pants I wore from before. This was never going to happen. I still owned the same belt from back then but had moved up two notches closer to the end. I was kneading the flab of my belly in front of the mirror, wishing I could fold it in some way to make it vanish. I would hate to dash her expectations.

I raked my fingers through my thinning hair. No greys. Creases formed around my eyes when I squinted. I think they always did that. There was a family of hairs growing out of my nose. I plucked them. A strange dark spot the size of a pea had appeared under my left ear.

I was closer to twenty-nine than thirty, so why did I think I was so old? At least I didn't have to wear glasses. My friends sharing this space never showed a concern over my age. It was one normal human condition I couldn't ignore. Forty or fifty years left for me, maybe a little more, that was nothing to them. Their timelessness taunted me every time I took notice of it. Their souls were in perpetuity. They never changed. Here I was, sporting spots and packing pounds. I had hairs migrating from my head to areas that didn't need them. What would happen if I fell ill? Would they know how to treat me? Would my dependence on modern medicine be the breaking point for the demon to cross the moat of flowers?

I was never more aware of my mortality than at that moment, staring at my reflection twenty minutes from midnight. I tucked my gut along with my shirt into my larger pants and buckled my belt.

"You look fine," Guff said from behind me. Inari approached as well. The past week had been tense, ticking off each day, then each hour. It was no wonder everyone jumped for the ceiling days prior when Colin knocked on the door. The aftereffects of that conversation still sat with me. A considerable part of me wanted to ask more from him. I wanted to know about that scar on his forehead, about the world I had pushed away, and about the ring on the wrong finger. What I really wanted was to prove it to him—to prove my sanity even at the cost of his.

"Is the time right?" Guff asked. I still hadn't said anything. A voice I rarely listened to was telling me not to go outside, not climb down that cove and wait until midnight. It was DOD's seed of doubt he had been germinating since arriving.   "Ten minutes," I said. The others had gathered as I made for the door. I threw on a beige cashmere jacket I had purchased several years ago.

"Pass me that coat please," I said to Guff, pointing to the worn heavy wool and polyester black long coat on the rack. Guff looked confused.

"You already have a coat," he said.

"It's for her."

"I made clothes to fit," Inari interjected. "Take them with you." I shook my head.

"It has meaning," I answered.

I opened the door and stood at the precipice. The waning moon was bright enough to cast a dim light on the distant cliffs. My eyes had yet to adjust so the cove was still a dark pit. I could hear the waves lapping across the rocks. I could feel the steady breeze that Elisa controlled. I placed a hand on the doorframe. I needed encouragement.

"She will come," Inari pushed. "William…"

I turned to her.

"She will come," she added.

I nodded and walked off the porch. I heard a second set of steps behind me. I turned around to Guff. Everyone else waited by the door.

"Guff?" I asked.

"Yes?"

"I can do this myself."

Guff looked back to the others at the door and then turned back to me.

"Yes," he said, "Yes, you can." We shook hands. "Good luck." He then turned back to the house. They offered me one final look before closing the door. I made my way to the cove.

As my eyes adapted, the sitting stone emerged from the darkness. It was still empty. Midnight waited patiently minutes away. A foolish thought, I wondered if it was midnight here or midnight in some other place. Which time zone did she follow? Was it Eastern Standard Time? What if I missed her?

"And when she doesn't come," a deep voice growled, "you'll know it was a waste, every moment of your life, every brick of that house, every nail hammered. What if the ocean offers you nothing? The water is spit. The cove is a maw which will swallow you."

I could see DOD at the edge of the cliff, within view but safely away. At this hour, he was merely a silhouette against a curtain of night.

"She'll be there," I answered.

"At the moment of midnight, I will count every second of every minute, each shout a mockery of your commitment. It will all be a waste. You will whither your years in a waking dream. Old and feeble, doctors will force you into a white cell with padded bedposts and bars on the windows. Your friends will not visit you. They'll hear about your fate, shake their heads, then forget about you and go about their day."

I ignored him and made my first step down to the cove. The germ will not take root.

"You think she would have shown some proof by now?" DOD screamed a moment before my head vanished from his view. I turned and stepped back up.

"What?" I asked.

"They can only take human form for a day every ten years." DOD lowered his voice, forcing me to step back up to hear him. "But she is still a creature of the ocean. Why hasn't her whiskered head poked above the water to reaffirm your conviction? Not one yelp, not one flipper flap. Surely she would have risen once by now, taken a fish from your hand."

There had to be a reason why. Perhaps it was forbidden. It would be simple enough to explain it as part of her convention. Perhaps she didn't want me to see her that way, to be so close and so distant. It would be painful for both of us.

"It was better not to see," DOD continued. "You seldom came to the rock. You walk the cove but never sat. You don't wait for a sign. You never did because you would wonder the same."

I looked back to the cove. I saw the soft waves rising up the rock. Five minutes.

"Maybe she does watch but can't bring herself to show me...knowing we can't be together." I don't know if I could bear to see the animal and not touch the woman. DOD was right with one point I couldn't deny. I would look from the upper floor of the house, I would walk the cove, but I never sat upon the rock, not since then. That spot was reserved for the both of us. It never felt right to sit there alone.

"Convenient," DOD answered, "impossible to prove. Never know for certain--"

"I do appreciate our conversations, DOD. Keeps me sharp. It's down to four minutes. I'm going to spend them at the rock. Don't suppose you could you offer some privacy."

DOD pushed back on his cane but kept himself planted. I turned back and proceeded down the incline.

"I'll crow when the clock strikes," DOD shouted out of sight.

Several patches of mould were sticking from cracks in the rock. Beyond that, it hadn't changed. I placed my black wool coat over the damp rock and found a comfortable position to wait. The rock had corners and angles I didn't recall it having.

I heard a splash and immediately jolted my head to focus on the source. My heart sank as I recognized the mermaid.

"Banya," I said, "How are you this evening?" She floated closer to the shore. I was trying not to focus on her exposed breasts.

"Ensuring the waters are calm and without predators," she answered. I smiled and nodded. "I have not seen her," she added. "But that means nothing to our kind. We are rarely ever seen by anyone."

"Thank you," I said. My building anxiety was engraved across my face. Banya dropped until only her head was in view.

"Ten years is an insignificant drop against the flow of time. We take these drops as our fortune. Treasure every second and horde it as a squirrel in winter. Don't rush these moments given to you." She dipped back into the water. I glimpsed her flopping tail as she disappeared. I check my watch and felt my stomach tightening.

One minute.

The waves felt louder than they had ever been. I tried to make out some disturbance, a shallow splash that could only have come from a smaller animal. I picked up the black coat, refolded it, and placed it back in the same spot. My fingers began tapping the rock.

The ocean was so vast. How far could she have travelled? What threats could there be that she had no influence over? I would see fishing boats on occasion from the house. They hated when they caught seals. It was a bad omen but it still happened from time to time.

Thirty seconds.

I felt my strength leave me. The tightness in my chest was growing worse. It worked itself to my limbs and they felt weak. My shoulders dropped. My arms fell limp at my side. I concentrated on keeping my breath deep and slow. I felt my pulse thump up my neck. I couldn't check the watch again. I waited. I thought it was past midnight. She hadn't arrived. I was expecting a taunt from over the cove. I didn't want to look at the watch. I needed to. Acting nonchalant, I lowered my head and turned my wrist around without lifting my arm.

At that second, it turned to midnight.

I looked up and saw her.

I almost fainted. I put an arm on the rock to prevent a stumble. The possibility that it was only a seal never occurred to me. It was her. The animal looked exactly as I remembered, black skin and long whiskers. She slithered across the surface until reaching the shore. The seal clumsily slumped upon the beach and approached me.

She was cautious. It looked as if she didn't recognize me. The seal knew I was familiar but didn't understand how or when. All it could feel was a sense of relief and trust.

I knew she would ask me to look away but I couldn't help but stare. To think there was once a germ of doubt.

She flopped a flipper over her eyes. I smiled, covered my face, and turned away. I felt the black coat slip from beside me. Her hand caressed mine a moment later. I slowly lowered my hand and turned to her, eyes still shut.

The weight in my heart still hadn't lifted. Not when I lifted my eyebrows. Not when I cracked one eye open and then followed with the other. Not when I saw her before me, wearing my coat, her face unchanged in all those years. She left the two top buttons undone. I suddenly felt ashamed at my accumulation of lines, marks, and spots that came with age. How dare I show the wear of time while she didn't?

She pulled her wet, dark hair from her face and curled it around her ear. Her blue eyes illuminated her rosy skin and her sprinkling of beige freckles. I still hadn't said anything. So much time had passed and she still could paralyze me.

"*Madainn mhath,*" She whispered.

"My father was Robert Weaver," I replied.

"I know," she answered. I rolled my hand to interlock with her accepting fingers.

"To the second."

"Felt a lifetime," she said.

"I never doubted." I would have admitted worry, but I never claimed it as doubt.

"I will admit uncertainty," she answered. "You are here."

I lifted one cheek to smile. "Seasoned, weathered somewhat." She reached up to caress my face, from the tip of my receding hairline to cup her fingers around my eye.

"Soul is unchanged. Nothing else matters."

We shared a kiss that lasted a full breath.

"And you're as I remember," I answered as I pulled away. "Exactly. I'll admit not knowing what to do next."

She kissed me again and I realized I was stupid for wondering about the next minute, or the minute after or the minute after that. We said nothing and I didn't care. All I could think about was the smell of her hair, the saltwater on her lips.

We parted and held an inch apart from our noses.

"The ocean felt empty," she said. "We carry little more than emotions from form to form. I remember our meeting as a fresh memory. Everything between was a dream. And when I take to water, I begin to forget the land.

"Somehow," she said as she rolled the back of her hand down my face, "I still remembered you." I could tell she was noticing the differences that came over time. If only I could have had the body of Colin, virtually unchanged in a decade. She didn't appear to mind. Her face never

revealed a flaw in her smile. Never once did I appear to dash her
expectations.

"I realize it was too much to ask," she said.

"What?" I asked. She pulled away.

"Everything you would sacrifice. All that would be required. It would
be too much. I fear I have done harm to you. What have you given up to
be here? What loves have you rejected? What futures have you refused?
So many prospects for one emerging to adulthood, why would you wait for
me?"

"You do yourself a disservice. There could have been prospects. I
might have had another future. But given the options, this was one choice
easily made. I have thought of little else." She was staring past my eyes. I
could tell her no lies and we both knew that.

"Not one love?" she asked with an almost pouty frown. It was
adorable.

"Despite temptations, there was never a threat."

"And have you considered beyond today? I could not."

"As promised," I said, "I own this land now. I never have to leave it."
Her mouth dropped and she looked about the cove. "Yes," I continued,
"the cove as well."

"And you have waited…alone?"

I chuckled. "There is much to tell you," I said. "Trust me, the time
flew."

Skye looked down to her left, to her sealskin firm in her hand. A
smile crept back to her face. She brought her coat to rest on her waist.

"You must take this from me," she said. "I cannot offer it." I paused.
Part of me disliked the idea of forcing the coat from her, but I understood

why. "Moments like this," she continued, "I despise the nonsense that binds me."

I placed my hand on the sealskin.

"I know," I replied. "I know of convention. I know of noegic. I know the questions without answers, explanations for things that don't exist. I know the *whos* and the *whats*. I know enough to not ask why. So don't break your own rules and ask me that, just as I won't ask why you would accept such an ordinary man. Do you wish me to take it?"

"I cannot say that. I will resist, regardless of my wishes."

I gripped her coat firmly and gave it a slight tug. She refused to release it. Her hands held on despite her soul telling them otherwise. Her shoulders were shaking as she fought off her compulsions. She released her fingers suddenly and she allowed the coat to fall away. I held it under an arm and tried to calm her. I held her until she stopped shaking. It wasn't a fear of me or of tomorrow. It was the uncertainty of happiness.

"Take my hand," I said. "I want to show you what you helped create."

I led her up the cove with our arms laced. She stumbled occasionally as she relearned walking. Before we reached the crest, her eyes quickly darted to the black figure at the edge of the dark field.

"Who is that?" she asked.

I gently encouraged her along, hoping she would focus back on me. The figure was tracking us, but he said nothing. He knew there was no point. I had scored for the winning team. There was no use in him disputing it. He stood silent, planning his next strategy.

"That's for later," I said. "One thing at a time."

We reached the top of the cove and Skye saw the house for the first time. In truth, the top floor had been visible since half way up the cove but she had been more concerned with watching her feet.

She was still settling from the astonishment that I had waited for her, that I had fulfilled what I had promised. She had expected a bungalow or a cottage. She was worth more than that.

"A mansion," she whispered

"As I promised."

She shook her head and squeezed my hand. It was euphoric.

"Too much to ask," she said.

"No, it wasn't."

"Too much to give."

"It was a bargain."

"You did it."

"A refuge...for you, me, and everyone else that sees what cannot be true." She pulled me close and leaned in as if it was a monster terrifying her. Had I gone too far? She wanted me a humble fisherman with a log cabin by the shore. She expected and was prepared for two or three rooms, a wood stove for cooking, maybe a boiler. She would sew and cook while I took a boat out to fish. I still didn't know how to swim. This palace was tall and clean, with a field of flowers that strangely kept in bloom at night. Every wall was infested with glass with lights and colors illuminating the night. Wood and stone radiated from it. A garden grew plentiful. A towering fan spun against the constant breeze.

"Are you frightened?" I asked.

"Yes...but not of you."

I wondered if she preferred isolation or had it forced on her. Was she worried I had planned to parade her in front of friends? Perhaps the house was simply too much of something. Too much peach, too much brick, perhaps it had to be made only of wood. Perhaps it couldn't be two floors. I never considered that.

"Please tell me what it is," I begged.

"Don't think me as unappreciative," she answered, focusing on me. "You are here. That's all that I needed." She was shivering, nervous over emotions she hadn't felt in hundreds of years. "Show me your house."

"It's actually yours." I guided her to the entrance.

Skye was shocked and fascinated at what greeted her. The others had discussed it amongst themselves and decided to keep mostly away, leaving only Inari, Guff, and Elisa in the hallway. Miran buzzed around, refusing to settle or be ignored. They all carried wide smiles and open arms.

"Welcome to the family, dear," Inari said, her tail intentionally coiled around her waist to be in view. Elisa hung off the side of Guff while drifting her legs behind her.

"Magnificent," was all Skye could manage. She instantly recognized foreign faces. I could see her slowly understanding without being told. The land was kissed by magic for she had bound herself to it. I had built a house in dedication to her, focusing that power. It would rise as a lighthouse for others to be drawn. Skye looked past the others and found even more fae poking from the cracks of doors and from distant rooms. There would not be an isolated life waiting for her. It wouldn't be the simple life of a fisherman's wife. I had taken on a crusade built upon the foundation of the union of two souls.

"Is this all that's left?" Skye whispered.

"I hope not," I answered.

"And you have done this?"

Inari answered for me. "He did everything for you."

Skye loosened her grip on my coat with one hand but kept the other interlocked with mine.

"A refuge not just for me," she said, "but for everyone. It is beyond any dream I could ever hope to have."

"As we always knew," Guff said, "You hit the pay dirt with this one."

"Welcome to your home," Elisa cheered as she floated closer. She brushed a hand over Skye's cheek.

"We need to get you proper clothes," Inari said.

"When she is ready," I said, "We'll move as fast as she wants to move."

Skye's smile finally returned with full vigor. She nodded to the group and then to me. The others moved in and greeted the new arrival. I announced their full names, allowing each resident to pay respects. I told Skye of the boogeyman under the house, the frightening spirit hiding in the corner, of the gargoyle squatting on the roof. I was quick in my explanations. I wanted to carry her away from the others, to hear just her voice, to feel just her touch. Inari knew this and after I had introduced them all, the kitsune stepped in front the others.

"It is too late to invest in further conversation," she said. "Let's give them the evening. We shall all retire." Inari turned to Skye. "I have guessed your shape but I must apologize. I hadn't expected you to be so...elfin. We can adjust them later. A wardrobe awaits you in the master room."

"Thank you for everything, dear elder," Skye said with a bowed head. Inari lifted Skye to look into the taller fae's eyes.

"It is a trifle compensation for what you have done for us. Your love has saved us all. A closet full of clothes hardly compares. It will be some time before we can repay you for what you have given us."

*

"I can feel the water," she whispered to me. We shared the swing on the second-floor terrace, overlooking the cove. She had changed into a double-layered white silk gown. I was cold with my triple layers but she showed no indication of feeling the chill. We huddled under a wool blanket overlooking the night.

"Wind kicks up from the shore," I replied as I punted the rail to rock the swing.

"Everything you built?" she asked.

"Not all. The swing's mine. I had help with the rest."

She pushed herself closer and flicked her tongue against my ear as she spoke.

"Tell me," she murmured. I didn't answer her immediately. The sensation of her fingers and tongue drew out my remaining sense of composure. I was desperate to maintain self-control. My blood was pumping and my appendages were getting stiff. I didn't know if she intended to test my resolve or break my spirit.

"W-What w-would you like me to t-tell you," I stuttered out.

"Every moment of your life before this one," she answered. I started to relax. I wrapped my arms around her as she dropped her head to my shoulder. I flicked my tongue across her ear as I answered.

"It began with you."

TWELVE

This chapter has been removed due to its subject matter.

THIRTEEN

Kira was four years old when we welcomed her baby brother.   She was born like her mother, with rules that disobeyed the normal world. Robert was ordinary, muscles and bones. Skye had asked what I wanted before their births. I told her I wouldn't answer that. Leave it up to chance.

Good answer.

I half expected Kira to emerge a seal. Her ears were pointed. Everything else was as her mother except for one thing. She had my eyes.

Robert had fair hair. There were no blondes in my family line. He had my thick brow and drooping cheeks. We decided to offer guardianship of the children to another resident in case of an unforeseen future. Inari was honored to be selected for Kira. Guff was deservedly chosen for Robert. Elisa was promised the third child even though Skye and I had decided not to have one.

The children were no accident. Skye chose the exact time of birth. Robert emerged with neither a whine nor a whimper. He practically fell into my arms and chuckled.

That may appear a strange delivery except that Kira, minutes after her birth, got up from the towels laid upon the bed and began running around the room. The umbilical cord flapped behind her as the infant jumped and dodged Inari's attempts to catch her. Elisa finally scooped up the child and handed her to her mother.

Kira never stopped running.

*

I had so many questions for Skye and knew I would never ask them all. If she had no language of her own, then in which language did she think? If under her skin, she was only emotions and actions, then how could we have children? Did I have a hand in making Kira that way or was the child another random assortment of rules that made no sense?

Those questions could never be answered. They could never be asked. I could never want to know. I didn't want, care, or need to.

I had picked up Gaelic but Skye never spoke it to me again. I always referred to her as Skye, never as Eileen. She never asked that I change that and I never bothered to bring it up. I assumed Eileen was a given name while Skye was a chosen one I had gotten to calling her. I could tell she enjoyed being called it, as it was unique and in disobedience of her convention. Perhaps there was room for minor rebellions against the rules that dictated her soul.

I admitted to her that I never learned to swim. She taught me. She had never eaten sushi. I made it. Our lives were saturated by moments like that. She could sew and I could cook. We never needed to do either. The other residents always saw to our needs. Skye tried to make herself productive but the others, even Inari, had elevated her to a higher status. She'd been made into an avatar, a symbol representing the power of the house and the protection it offered.

I thought those first days would be marked by concern about the coming mornings. Each day I woke, she was still there. We hadn't left the bedroom and terrace for nearly a month. I was surprised, given her energy and my enthusiasm, that we didn't sire an entire family of selkies, kitsune, elves, and boggles.

Guff remarked later that all those were possibilities. He added, "It was a minor miracle she didn't fire out an entire litter then and there."

*

Kira stormed into the bedroom after being given the "all-clear" from Inari. The child never slept. Robert was still asleep in the next room. The buoyant girl looked nearly eight though I knew she was nowhere close to that.

"Mother, Father," Kira exclaimed. She leapt upon the bed and ran up between us. We had been up for several moments but had been enjoying the silent morning until then. Kira dropped on her knees and was obviously excited about something trivial. Every morning, she would exclaim to everyone that would listen about how amazing something inconsequential was. Yesterday, a butterfly landed beside her while she tended the garden with Pixis. The bug didn't fly away for ten minutes. Before that, a bright red leaf fell onto her lap while she was reading a book alongside Lazarus on the roof. The irony was not lost on me.

Her mother held a finger to her lips and the child went silent. Skye then moved her finger up and brushed aside her daughter's hair.

"Thank you, mother," Kira said. She ran enthusiastically out of the room. When allowed, Kira would vanish into the purple flowers. We wouldn't see her for hours. When he got older, Robert would surely ask why his eccentric sister was free to do anything while he was burdened with limits. I would tell him then that Kira could never leave the house and the surrounding land while he could travel the world if he wished it. While young, we imposed rules. As he aged, he would be freer than anyone.

"She must get that from her mother," I joked to Skye after our daughter had left. "No crazy fairies on my side."

Skye laughed and pushed her back against my chest. I curled my arms around her and weaved our legs together.

"Would you have preferred something with wings?" she replied as she squeezed her head under my chin.

"Didn't know you had say in that," I whispered.

"Not saying I did. Never tried it before. There is still something about her that reminds me she is mine."

"Well, I hope so." I realized she wasn't joking. I loosened my grip and pulled her around to face me. "You were concerned about that. That what emerged would not be related to you."

"Beauty siring beasts, it has happened," she replied. "More often than not. There is always a loyalty with our lineage, but I have seen the kindest of souls beget monsters. Faeries into dragons." We could hear Kira outside, frolicking near the house with Miran and Pixis. Pixis was a best friend and confidant of all childish secrets. Miran tagged along out of boredom. Pixis had sworn to Miran that if she harmed Kira in any way, the dawnling would rip off the fairy's wings. That threat never worked with me but Miran never touched Kira after that.

"Then I guess we can count ourselves fortunate," I said to Skye against the backdrop of childish laughter.

"I think that is from you," Skye replied.

"What?"

"Your contribution. If you cannot see anything else in her, see that she is what we wish—gentle, curious. Worthy offspring. It perhaps explains why so many of us prefer to attract your kind." She caressed my chin when she said it. That pulled blood from my brain.

"Not all of them," I said. "So many flee, or worse, lure them to be prey." I was relieved no flesh eaters ever showed up at the house. There would be no way to know. As Inari had once explained, some of the greatest of monsters had the most pleasing appearances. I had read the tales but never met them for real.

"You weren't concerned at all were you?" Skye teased.

"Of you? The only time I was frightened was when I might have lost you."

She inched away from me. Her persuasive touches and luring strokes stopped. Her eyes fell off me and she contemplated the future rather than the past. When I had said it, I realized what was implied. I hadn't seen the calendar in weeks. We never checked the days off. We never marked the passage of time beyond birthdays. We didn't want to be reminded of how it would end. Time itself had melted its hours and minutes into a single unbroken moment ten years long.

"I know what you're thinking," I whispered calmly to her.

"Life," she answered.

"I thought ten years would be a long time. It wasn't." I seldom looked into the mirror other than to shave. The hair was growing greyer and thinner. I hadn't gained any more weight or any more spots. My skin felt rough, peppered with minuscule pits and valleys. Skye hadn't aged a second from the first time I saw her at the cove. Kira raced towards adulthood but eventually, at some point, she would just stop. It could be in five years or ten or twenty. We didn't know, as her complete convention was still a mystery to us. Robert was a slave to time as I.

"So many loves collapse under their own weight," I said. "At least with us, we'll never know gravity's effect."

"I would have liked to have known," she whispered.

We heard the quick yelps of an impatient infant next door. He wailed like a normal child. Skye was vulnerable upon hearing Robert's howl. No magic or wishing could soothe him. She felt powerless against his juvenile concerns. I always attended to him first. If it was for feeding, I called his mother. With Kira, Skye understood her intent before speaking, but with Robert, she was puzzled by his sudden mood swings.

Dealing with the first diaper had me laughing days after. Kira would eat but never need a change. Like her mother, many of the details were kept out of the stories. I kissed Skye on the cheek, rolled from the bed, and attended to my son.

*

It was a casual look outside the drapes. Skye wasn't in the house but that had never concerned me before. I screamed when I noticed her talking to DOD. What could be going through her mind? I knew we didn't have long but this wasn't the solution to anything. Kareen had followed me out with more sure to follow.

"Skye!" I shouted to her. "Skye! What are you doing?" She was inches from DOD's reach. The edge of the property always seemed so close but at this moment, it appeared to stretch to the vanishing point. As I ran, it felt like the terrain was sliding backward, keeping me where I was. She seemed unafraid. Her bare feet and legs visible as her lilac sundress fluttered in the breeze.

As the periphery of purple blossoms approached, I noticed Skye turning to offer a mild smirk. That didn't help at all.

"Talking to your friend," Skye said to me. I grabbed her arm as hard as I ever had. I pulled her back and pushed myself into the crossfire. I was frightened and angry. Part of me wanted to carry Skye back to the house like an arrogant knight treating his spoils. The other half wanted to assault the beast. I had never touched him in all these years. Something always prevented me.

"He is hardly my friend," I snapped.

"He is the demon on your shoulder," Skye said. I released her but she continued to hold onto me. "He knows so very much about you."

"Unfortunately." I gently coaxed her further from the demon. She knew she was safe. She might have encountered his kind before and knew his limits. My heart was still racing. I tried to shield that with calm conversation. "So would you be the angel?"

"Perhaps. If so, it is good that we three can talk."

"Yes," DOD hissed, "How very...productive." I turned my head to him and saw a smile that bisected his face.

"It's only a shame I didn't buy more property," I retorted, still encouraging Skye to keep her distance. She orbited me and pulled away.

"You shouldn't hate him," she said.

"Kind of hard to not to."

"He is a slave as we are...worse so, as his convention ultimately leads to suicide. The only one of us that has that. Even Lows of Lakesides pities such a curse."

We circled each other as I placed myself between them again. At the very least, I needed to keep her away to prevent the others from needlessly placing themselves at risk. Guff was the type of unnecessary hero to risk his own life if he thought Skye was under threat.

"Even still, despite your freedom, you being so close to him bothers me. You might know his reach but I don't and DOD is the villain in this tale. He is not one to share tea with."

"Well, you are correct. I know his grasp and what he can do. I have seen his like kill hundreds of my kind. So part of me offers compassion while another takes joy in your protection. I remain out here to remind him and me of why we are here."

The others were running out. I gently offered a palm to communicate our safety. They didn't slow.

"You have nothing to volunteer?" I asked my silent nemesis behind me.

"It would serve no purpose," DOD answered.

I gave Skye a look she understood. She caressed a finger around my chin and then leaned out to speak to DOD.

"Pleasant talking to you." She then laced her arm around mine and pulled me gently back to the others and our house.

"What were you discussing?" I whispered to her.

"Mostly you. He does know you better than most. I wanted to learn more."

"You only need to ask."

"I know, but as I said, I had pity for him. That moment is over."

Well, in the future, be careful. The last thing we need is Kira trying to do the same."

"I know...I am sorry." She pushed herself close. "Perhaps there will be a time we will not fear him."

*

As Skye fed Robert on the terrace, I enjoyed the seawater on my toes, sitting in front of the large rock. My daughter splashed and pranced barefoot up to her knees in placid tides. She flicked her fingertips across the surface like a flapping bird. Earlier, I had made myself look at the calendar and note the day, month, and year. Skye's conversation with DOD was a symptom of a trend I had been seeing with her. It was the misdirected actions of a person contemplating suicide.

Her convention would force her departure, but as it was part of her, it would still be her choice. What a malicious compulsion to force actions upon her and make it seem it was her idea. She was breaking her ties and preparing for the end. Taking to the sea would end this life. It was feeling as callous to her as taking a razor to her wrist or hanging from a rope from the terrace in front of her children. I started to feel guilty, about providing a life that she would be compelled willingly to surrender.

"What bothers you, papa?" Kira asked me after a splash.

I had rested my head back upon the stone and half-closed my eyes.

"How can you read me so well?" I replied. Kira stopped cavorting and swiveled towards me, resting her hands on the waistline of her lavender sundress, nearly identical to her mother's.

"Would you rather I act the child?" she asked, her juvenile tone vanishing instantly.

"The future, honey."

"More years ahead than behind. That's what Inari told me."

"Well," I groaned and looked up to the overcast sun, "she is right in that. Though that may be true for the universe, it's not always true with people."

Kira let her arms loose and twirled them around, slapping the surface of the water as she did. She stopped upon noticing the returning trawler drifting by the bay. It was a rare site. The number of passing boats and cars had decreased each year. That was the first we had seen in two months.

"Look, a boat!" Kira shouted happily again as the child she pretended to be. "Can I swim to it? I can make them not see me."

My eyes opened and I stared at her. I knew she was mine. I could see and feel the connection. We had guessed or noticed the details of her convention. There was still some doubt. She couldn't change to an animal, that much we knew.

A maturity within her made her speak older than even Elisa when the need arose. She would then remember her role and revert to the child we expected her to be. It was like she was an adult trapped in a child's body, but enjoying the part she was expected to play.

"Can you?" I asked her.

"My hair would look like seaweed," she revealed.

"When did you learn that?"

"Never."

I could see her already being caught in a net and dragged onto a boat to be exploited. I remembered only briefly the legend of a water spirit that only appeared as its body lifted from the water. Under the surface, only its hair was perceptible as kelp. I couldn't remember anything else about the myth although I was certain that it was probably a "she" and was probably naked.

I had already noticed this several years ago while giving her a bath, as her bottom half vanished under the surface. We felt it best she discover this naturally on her own.

"You have to learn to be careful when we are not around," I said. "You have to learn to be cautious."

"I don't like fear," she said in passing as he stared at her submerged and invisible feet.

"Neither do I," I answered, "but it happens." I had no idea where DOD was. I couldn't see him from atop the cove. This was usual for him, as he had stopped following me around the property some years ago. "It's right to fear the monster that watches us because we have reason to. Don't fear the water or the wind. Not the night. Even if you can appear as cloth in wind or weeds in water, don't try to sneak past him. You are bound to this land, Kira."

"I know. I don't envy the world outside. All I need is here." She walked onto the shore. I offered her a towel to dry. Her skin hadn't pruned.

"Your brother may not agree," I said. "He is normal...and a normal world may call him. There may come a time when you will inherit all this."

"Why would I?" she said as she sat next to me. I offered my arm around her shoulders.

"Because unlike you, there's probably less time ahead of me than behind."

"And mother will go too."

I cracked my mouth to answer but could only exhale. She knew the rules without being told. I didn't know what she implied. Was Kira expecting or hoping I would burn the sealskin? Did she assume I would stand helpless as her mother escaped this prison and returned to the sea?

Kira spoke up again, "She will age like you."

"What do you mean?" I whispered.

"I have seen her weeping by the water. I asked her why. She said she was saying goodbye."

"She means to stay?"

"And then grow old."

I nodded but wasn't agreeing. We spent an hour in silence looking across the rolling waves. After the boat had passed, we saw no others.

*

Skye and I had avoided the conversation for years and our skills at distraction were improving. On the few times I had gathered the courage to air out the obvious, she would touch me in places that instantly cleared my head of all concerns. It was the day before the anniversary, before ten years had raced by, when she finally volunteered the subject herself.

"Felt too quick," Skye said. "Each memory is still vivid." We shared the last morning drifting over the violet countryside, circumnavigating the entire property as close to the edge we dared to walk. Hands firmly interlocked.

"And hopefully it will remain so," I replied. I made a decision from two less than favorable possibilities. As I continued to reflect on my choice, however, the path became more a certainty. Neither option had filled me with joy. One held immediate gratification with an end marred in misery. The other, the one I had endorsed, kept her spirit untarnished at the cost of my own. "Guff has kept your skin under lock. It is waiting for you."

"I want you to burn it," Skye replied. Despite what Kira had said, I needed Skye to say it. As she did, my decision became resolute.

"You'd become mortal," I replied.

"A trivial expense," she said. I stopped walking. Pulling her arm. Turning her to face me.

"I don't think so. You'd be tied to a mortal existence. You'd lose your ties to Kira, which I know is very special to you."

"She would still be my child as she is yours."

"But you're immortal. You'll always be here. You don't want the possibility of a mortal soul hanging over you."

She fell into my arms.

"I cannot bear to be without you. Without our children. No ocean is vast enough to compare. Take the skin to the roof and burn it to ash."

"No," I said. My stomach was twisting. A sharp pain was crawling up my spine, headed for my brain. I had to think of her and the future, of our kids.

"I cannot do this," she cried. "Only you can."

"It's spiteful."

"But I ask you," she said. I held her head in my hands and gently kissed her on the forehead.

"And I love you for offering…but I can't take away what you are."

"But we could travel to the city. You can show me your world." There was an appeal but I knew she had seen plenty from the water. It was a selfless offer on her part, hoping I would accept.

"It's not much to speak of," I said.

"I cannot return if I leave. I will be bound to the sea for the rest of your life."

"I know. But our children will never fear the sea. They will always carry a bond to it that can never be broken. They will remember you as you are. They will always know you live. They would never see you grow old, take on some condition that makes you forget them. You will always be near, even if they don't see you. I could never bear to take the magic from you."

"It is more than our children," she said.

I had hoped to keep it with them but Skye knew me well enough to read past that. Kira and Robert only partially factored in my decision. Robert would never remember his mother as I did. He would only know recollections. Legends authenticated. Myths believed to be true. For the real son of a magical being, I still felt those appropriate memories to have. The real reason was more personal.

"Could you bear to see me age?" I asked her. "Could you see me with wrinkled and tattered skin? Glints of silver to a full beard of grey? My vision would go. My hearing would fail. I would kink my back, rest on a cane, and remember nimbler times." I stroked her hair behind her ear. She pulled my hand from her face and held it to her heart.

"You still assume me some superficial nymph. You know I don't judge over such physical qualities. I want a life, not memories of another love that I'll languish over for a thousand years."

"But one of us would still see the other die. Could you see my existence crumble into brittle bones and short breaths? Our children would see the passing of both parents. It would be slow and unplanned. I would rather they see only one of us fade that way. I would like them to remember the magic of their mother, even if it's only from stories. And after I take my final dance, you would be able to return."

She could make a counterargument of equal weight. She would never see Robert grow through the trials and wonders of human life. I had to believe such a bond would carry through to her other life. If she could keep a fragment of our single day over a decade, than what we'd accomplished was sure to stay with her. I could tell Skye wasn't so certain. I could tell she was getting angry, just not with me.

"I hated your fairy tales," she protested. "If there was a knight and a maiden, some farmer's girl and her prince, it was always happily ever after. The story would close with a smile on the face of the reader. Never for us. Faeries, elves, spirits, we were all fated for misery. One side would die. They would run away. Be cast out. If you told the story to children, you would keep to the best parts. The teller would avoid the final page. The old stories--the first ones--they always forced my kind to a wretched end. Joy...was never permitted. Why can't one of us have a *happily ever after*?"

I knew she didn't want to grow old anymore than I wanted to. Even when I died at my scheduled time, when mortality deemed it necessary and needlessly ordinary, she would still have our children. After my last breath was taken, she would be permitted to return. She could see her children and grandchildren and every generation for one day every ten years as long as the house remained.

I felt my life ending with her taking to the sea. The sooner I shuffled off this existence, the sooner she could return to see her children. See what Robert had grown into, what random rules Kira had developed.

"You don't want to die with me," I forced myself to say. "I can't let you go that way. I just wish that you take more with you into the sea than just a dream. Take our life, the memories of land; show me you still exist out there. I'll accept the animal knowing you still swim."

"I'll take it all with me. Every moment."

*

She cuddled with Robert until the afternoon, until he fell asleep in her arms. Skye let drop a single tear, which rolled down her cheek and down Robert's forehead. As it fell into her son's eye, it turned the white of that one eye blue, a trait he kept for his life.

There was no formal goodbye to her daughter. In Kira's eyes, her mother wasn't going anywhere. She had no comprehension of the difference in physical forms. Given our daughter was gifted with immortality like the rest of the fae, the handful of years she would be away was inconsequential.

For the last few hours, the other fae had emptied the house and spent the evening in the shade of the eastern wall. This left the only time in our life where Skye and I had dinner alone. There was rice and fish, ginger sauce and sweet peppers, all spiced with the best the world, and Kareen, could provide. We studied each other's faces, trying our best to commit them to memory. I knew hers well, as it hadn't changed one blemish or wrinkle since the day I painted it.

We never needed words to tell the other what he or she liked. We took to the bedroom and said even less until the night had fully fallen. We raced through every pleasure the other wished until our stamina and imagination wells had dried up.

Afterward, I left her on the bed and found the wooden lockbox where Guff had placed Skye's coat. It was in the loft, behind a false wall, at the head of the bed Kira never slept in. It hadn't jostled an inch since Guff hid it there. It was necessary to do so. Despite desires to stay, if Skye knew where the coat was, she would take the skin and return to the water instantly, as was her compulsion. She could decide not to look for it. I still felt that if she knew, she could overcome such obligations. The others assured me that would not be the case. Skye never asked and I never told her. The spot was an easy one, as there weren't many hidden areas to stash such a box. Skye could have found it if she bothered to look. If she wanted to. The compulsion was specific—she would retrieve it if she stumbled upon it, was told were it was, or offered it back. It never specified that she seek it out.

I rolled the digits on the combination lock and opened the maple box originally designed to hold fishing rods. I had half expected that it wouldn't be there, that perhaps Skye had found it and burned it without telling me. Perhaps one from the house had moved it to prevent a change to the status quo. But there it was, unchanged. I checked my watch.

It was ten minutes to midnight.

I returned to the bedroom but found Skye gone. Although for a brief moment, I considered she had fled to avoid her fate, I knew she was waiting for me at the cove. She had taken my black cotton long coat. I finished dressing and made for the water.

She sat alone on the rock. I looked around the rim of the cliff. DOD was near, at the edge of the flowers. We didn't speak. I looked down to Skye and slowly made my way down the cove. As I did, DOD bowed his head and turned away. He walked back to the far side of the property.

"Promise me you will take them to water often," Skye whispered to me as I sat beside her.

"Every day," I replied. She kept her eyes to the sea. One part of her desired the sea and was pulling her back. If Skye could, she would tear herself in two.

I revealed her sealskin from behind me and placed it gently on her lap. She took it immediately from me and stood up. Her legs gave out slightly and she stumbled. I caught her shoulders and she let my coat fall off her naked body.

"And one more pledge," she told me. "When you feel your last hours slipping away, and you know the end is near, take to the sea...and I will find you."

"I promise it."

I released her and she stepped away from me. She dropped a foot into the rising wave. I know she would expect me to look away from her as she changed but I wouldn't this time. I needed to see her leave. Just beyond arm's length, she turned slowly back to me. She fell back into me and we kissed a last lasting time.

"You are such a man, William Weaver," she said.

Skye pulled away from me and drifted back into the water, up to her knees, her waist, all the time keeping her eyes focused on mine. Up to her shoulders. Up to her neck. Her chin touched the water and she dove under the layer. A half-moment later, the seal leapt into the air, encouraging me to smile. The animal paddled around the cove, splashing its flipper my way.

It knew me.

It remembered.

It stopped and treaded the water, staring back longer than a normal animal should. Such inhuman eyes and I could see the pain it felt upon recognizing me. It turned around and dove deep into the water.

I remained sitting on the rock until the dawn.

FOURTEEN

"What is this?" DOD asked me as I unfolded the worn burgundy poker table in front of him. I had used it as a worktable for my paints and brushes. It was seasoned by a spattering of various matted colors. A few fallen knives had scored the plastic surface.

"A folding table," I answered as I locked the legs into place. "Been around since the 19th century would be my guess." I pulled out the folding chair and followed suit. "Not really the beacon of progress but you should still recognize it." I placed the table on the periphery of flowers with one chair over blossoms and the other over grass.

"And its purpose," DOD asked, looming from his height. I sat on my side but he, rather it, remained standing.

"Funny you mention that. Rather surprised by your query. Everything must have a purpose. That's the one leg I have still in your world. I have a purpose. Like my paintings, I always wanted to be productive. It was when I stopped being productive in my paintings when I started to find a purpose."

He hadn't done much since Skye left. I had scored a victory in our undeclared war. My memories of her were vivid and virgin. He knew there was no way he would be able to stain those thoughts.

"That irony is only now dawning on me," I continued. "I imagine you're not a fan of art. A table, however, that's a purpose that never needs stating. Like the chair. As long as there are people, they will always need chairs and tables."

DOD still hadn't taken the seat.

"What a winded answer for a simple question," he said.

"Especially considering the answer was obvious," I replied. "It's not like I'm going to be entertaining guests here. Two chairs would indicate one for you and one for me."

"You're taunting me…daring me to offer that one insurmountable argument you cannot deny."

I should have brought tea or a chess set. The table was an implied shield. I should have concealed it with the impression of a function.

"It's been nearly twenty years since you've arrived, I said. "Figured you would have brought it up by now. You don't seem to be one to keep an ace this long."

"Your son," DOD said slowly.

"Son?" I snapped. DOD puckered the seam in his face as he smirked. He stepped around the chair and sat. He placed his elbows on the burgundy poker table and interlocked his spindly fingers.

"Your daughter you imagined as fae, so she cannot leave," he said. "Your son was created as flesh, but if he is part of your mind, then he is as susceptible to my wrath as any others in that house. According to your logic, I cannot touch him as I cannot touch you. So bring him out. Let me see him. Make him walk beyond the flowers. Test your theory. If he is of flesh, then I cannot harm him. But if he is a figment like everything else, then I can destroy him, and shatter this illusion in an instant.

The threat as made brought an instant apprehension, which DOD immediately picked up. His smile widened and he leaned in.

"And you immediately defend your offspring," he continued, "but that would mean you fear his life. If you fear his life then he must not be real. If he is not real, then none of it is."

"My apprehension is a reflex action," I retorted. My attempt at civility wasn't going to work. I was surprised it took him this long to try to bring my children into it. He never did when Skye was here. Even when they shared that moment near the end, he made no threats. If I didn't know better, it almost appeared as if he was apprehensive.

"Meaning there remains still a morsel of doubt on which I feed," DOD said.

"Of course, you put me in a bind," I replied. "If I refuse, then it will always haunt me and like cancer, it'll grow. And since you suggested it, I should assume you hope I'll flinch. Of course, you could be bluffing and I could call you on it. You're taking an equal risk."

"Assuming it's a bluff."

"I mean, if I present my son, and you do nothing, then it's validation that'll comfort me for the rest of my days." I was trying to sound nonchalant, but I knew he could read me. What if DOD had a power over mortals I was not aware of? Perhaps he could always harm me but never bothered. Even knowing my son was real, I could still be putting him at risk. I also was considering the fear DOD would put into Robert. He was only eight. "In fact, if you were a figment, you would die along with my son, as every dream would shatter at once. But if he survives, then you would survive…and be cursed to try a new approach, considering the last one you dogged after for so long would suddenly became moot."

"But I was the one that suggested it," DOD countered. "The fact you never did indicates you secretly feared I would bring it up. But now the chips are on the table…what pleasant timing for a prop to use." DOD rattled his withered fingers across the linoleum-textured surface. "I have cornered your king. Will you risk your pawn or will you forfeit?"

"Interesting point," I replied, "you bringing up strategy. If you are a disciple—-rather an avatar--of a technological world, then you are bound to explain everything. You expect me to make the logical choice, to protect my son. You're trying to gauge your opponent. Well, I'm not good at chess. I don't think two moves ahead. I think one."

I stood up and walked from the table. I didn't look back. I had the power to protect the house long after my passing. Proving to DOD would fortify my resolve and the defenses of my fortress long past my death. It would take root into the minds of those that rely on those walls.

I was going to end this once and for all.

*

Robert's brain was not just a dry sponge. It was an entire African saltpan like the Makgadikgadi…that was then covered in sponges. He remembered every fact and every myth I exposed him to. I handled his education precariously. He understood the balance of the two worlds and the importance of the house. Despite an obvious counterargument, I still felt it important to instruct Robert in everything I knew about science and history. The problem wasn't knowledge, as I told him, but in the need of outsiders following science to explain something that couldn't exist. I told him about what was real, what he could explain and what he could never.

I gently encouraged Robert to take the kitchen chair across from me. I sat down and acted as if his puppy just died.

"The man in black wants to meet you," I said to him.

"Why?" my son asked.

"Because he believes I will not let you walk outside the field of flowers," I said. "He believes you to be part of this world and not of the other one." I didn't indicate to which worlds I was referring. "He believes I won't allow you to leave because of fear he'd be able to harm you, despite you being like me."

"Let me," Robert answered. "I've always wanted to explore."

I held my son firmly by the shoulders. "I have never intended to keep you away. It just never occurred to me."

"I can do it," Robert reaffirmed. "I want to see more of the world. I want to walk around. I want to take a boat. Ride a bus." Robert turned to the floating nymph that drifted to overhear. "Tell him, Elise. I am brave."

Elisa placed a hand upon my shoulder. "He is very strong, William." She always supported him. Elisa had almost taken on a motherly role in her attention to Robert. I knew she was thinking of something else and was waiting for only a few more years. The prospect still bothered me.

"You would support this?" I asked her.

"He has nothing to fear," she said. "Do you have something to fear?"

I addressed my son again. I leaned, pulling Elisa with me. "He may frighten you. In fact, I'm sure he will. He'll make it seem like he'll hurt you. He'll make me worry that he can."

"But, he can't," Robert interjected.

"No...He can't." There it was. A moment of apprehension. That one moment where a part of me wasn't sure. If DOD tore apart my son, it would be that one moment that would crush the foundation of my life. The walls of the house would collapse seconds later. If I refused, then my son would do it on his own in time. Unless he was a figment. Then he would only do as I desired. He would never risk his life.

But my son wanted to. He wanted to do this. Did that part of me want this to end? Was part of me defiant of the truth until the bitter end?

"Just remember, he can't hurt you," I said. "You've been scared far worse around here. There's nothing out there you haven't seen before."

"I can do it," Robert repeated. I nodded and released him. Robert looked up to Elisa to read her approval. She drifted forward and kissed him on the cheek.

"Ewww...yucky," Robert squirmed as he wiped off his face. Elisa smirked and swam from the room.

"Yucky?" I whispered to him.

"She is neat and all, but Elise is weird."

"Give it a few more years, you may change your mind about that."

Robert jumped off the chair and followed me out. We made sure the others didn't see us leave. This was a private affair and I preferred us not having an audience.

"She is very," Robert added, "clingy."

"Clingy?" I asked.

"Like a sock in a dryer."

I didn't comment further. I didn't say anything at all until we had left the house. I held his hand as he skipped through the violet field. We approached the worn folding table and the stalky figure standing beside it, inches away from the furthest flower. No words were spoken until we were standing at the cusp of the border.

"Hello boy," DOD hissed.

Robert looked to me and whispered, "He's tall."

"Let that be the only thing he has over you," I replied.

"Did he tell you?" DOD asked. "Your life is in danger this close."

"You are the monster that wants to eat the others in the house," Robert said

"Just as I will devour you," was DOD's sinister serpentine threat.

Robert appeared unphased but I could feel him tightening his grip. His voice didn't show it. "I was told you cannot harm normal people."

"Who claims you to be normal?" DOD asked.

"My father and my father is right with everything."

"How could you be normal if your mother was not?"

"Because that's how it is, and there is nothing else to say about that."

I smiled proudly. Despite his education and the preaching I gave often, I was never sure Robert ever fully understood. His grip on my hand loosened but still held.

"But you fear me," DOD stated.

"Because you're still a stranger, and being my age, I'm allowed to be scared of you."

DOD looked up to me. "Notice how he doesn't talk like a normal child."

"He's mine," I retorted, "so obviously I'll allege him as being unique and gifted."

DOD stepped forward and addressed Robert. "He believes I cannot hurt you because, despite your mother, you are still presented as human."

"I am human," Robert replied.

"Prove it then. Step beyond the field flowers. Step from your father's world into mine, and prove yourself of flesh."

Robert looked at me and loosened his grip. I kneeled down to him. "I placed you here, Robert," I said. "Whichever step you take, I will support you. If you don't want to, you don't have to."

Robert stepped away from me and offered an unyielding stare to the demon. I immediately considered that Robert was probably too young. DOD would surely frighten the youth and that trauma could carry with him for years. Yet, my son had weathered so much so soon. He was raised believing in monsters. The goblin in the shadows was really there. What fantasies would a boy like that require?

He still had an imaginary friend. There was still room for that silent undemanding, ever-loyal confidant. Robert's was a miniature dragon named Bobby. When he first told me about it, I was actually convinced it was real.

Fear came from ignorance, of not knowing what was there. Once Robert knew the boogeyman's name, knew what he could do, Robert stopped being afraid. He believed me. That DOD was a threat only to the fairy world and not to us. Robert believed that despite DOD's threats, humans were immune to his evil.

Robert stepped outside the flowers. He was immediately snatched up by the imposing figure.

"Dad?" Robert shouted. He was afraid.

"It's going to be ok, son," I shouted back.

"Are you ready to face reality now, William?" DOD hissed. Robert was quivery as he was brought closer to the demon's peeling mouth. Something prevented me from wrestling my son from the monster. I had never touched the beast, not once. There had to be a reason for that. Perhaps that was part of his convention, one I could not fight against. He could touch but not be touched.

"Release him," I ordered.

"Maybe I will make it a long meal," DOD growled as he split apart his face. Robert closed his eyes and a drop ran down from his brown-in-blue eye. The demon bellowed with the lungs of an elephant.

I could hear Robert whispering to himself repeatedly. The mantra of denial. It would not hurt him. It would not hurt him. He had faith in his father's words.

"Release him!" I barked. DOD's jaw snapped shut.

"You think I intended to destroy him."

"What?"

"You would wall yourself into your world deeper than before. You would erase this memory and construct something favorable. Destroying this figment would be worthless." He twirled Robert around to face me but kept his tight grip on my son.

"It's just an excuse," I replied, "like everything else you have said.

"If I wanted to destroy your son, I would have done it the dozen times he had already snuck away."

"What?" I asked. Robert cracked an eye. He squirmed and his mouth warped like a Peanuts character.

"Sorry, Dad," Robert whimpered.

"I only wanted his scream," DOD snarled. "You didn't know? A boogeyman may feed on fear, but he is also compelled to protect those he sleeps under."

A dark shape passed over me. Spidery legs the lengths of telephone poles crushed over flowers. Leon, looking like a parade balloon from Pink Floyd's The Wall, marched from his protective shadow. His arms outstretched would touch either end of the property. They pulled Robert away with one clutch and with the other, picked up the expecting demon.

"No, Leon!" I shouted.

"You will no longer...be tolerated here," the boogeyman hissed. "Enjoy...the walk."

The demon's jaw cracked open. It glowed and began to shred Leon apart. Before fully tearing him to shreds, the fairy hurled the demon over the western horizon. At that speed and altitude, he surely hit water. The process of Leon's destruction continued and the body vanished into loose strands of cloth. The gangly legs toppled like felled trees back to the Earth.

I caught my son as the disconnect hand released him. Robert was crying, but not from fear.

"Oh no, Leon," Robert whimpered. I held him tight.

"It's okay," I said. "Look at me. Look at me. It wasn't your fault."

"I should have told you I had snuck away," he cried.

"It's okay. I knew you had. It's what boys do."

Guff embraced us both as the others surveyed the horror of fallen limbs.

"What happened?" Guff said.

"Leon is gone," I said, "so is DOD. At least, for a while."

"Why?"

"Because," I said, still holding onto my wailing son, "because the house is real. Everything here is."

*

"Dad?" My son asked me, weeks later. I had just tucked him in. Filling every vertical face in the room were dozens of his paintings. A blossoming skill that would surely surpass my own in a few years.

"Yes, Robert," I answered, taking my seat on the corner of his bed.

"Why you?"

"Why me what?"

"Why did this happen to you?" he asked. "Why did you and mother meet right then and there?"

"I thought about that occasionally, but once you start wondering why, you have to acknowledge that there is a reason."

"But you have explained other things."

"Because asking those questions and knowing those answers won't destroy what you're observing."

"But what came before mother?"

"Her mother."

"And before that?" Robert persisted, lifting himself to the bed's headboard. "When does it stop?"

"Whenever it does."

"But something just cannot come from nothing."

Usually, a parent would answer such inquisition. It was natural. How could I break that? Robert believed in both worlds, but he felt compelled to know why and how. Thousands of years ago, and even still today, parents placed a higher intelligence as the source of creation. For an imaginative mind like a child's, it's an easy answer. Eventually, science replaced many of these explanations. Both of these justifications offered counterarguments for every loophole that popped up. One demanded faith. The other demanded fact. Neither of which was required for this world. How would I explain that to him?

"Science can get to a fraction of a fraction of a fraction of a second before the beginning of our universe," I said. "Yet it still can't explain the second before. Your mother and her kind have the same issue."

"What about a magic man?" Robert said.

"Magic man?"

"Well, if they can create something from nothing, why couldn't someone create everything from nothing?" Magic man, I wished that's all it was. I wished there was no corruption or conflict related to such an innocent possibility. Just a magic man and leave it at that.

"You see, that's the real dilemma," I answered. "People have wondered about the reasons of things since the moment they began thinking outside of food and shelter. Without knowing anything about gravity or particle physics, they imagined great minds floating out of sight that created and controlled everything that wasn't us...and sometimes us as well. I honestly don't know how mother and her kind fall in on this. When I read about those books about gods and the games they played, I figured they were just exaggerated stories from unencumbered imaginations."

"Unencumbered," Robert asked.

I smiled. "Funny how that was the only word that confused you." I patted him on his lap. "Don't worry about it. Anyway, they and us lived together until we created gods to explain them. When that proved ineffective, we turned to science. I don't blame either. It would be like punishing the scorpion for stinging the turtle. It's in his nature."

"Scorpion stinging a turtle?"

"Old story, I'll tell you later. We, being men, have to fight that urge to explain it, less we remove the power of the house and the shelter we provide them. That's important, Robert, if you decide to go out and see the world without me, you must know that no explanation is worth losing what we have here. If you want a fantasy world, you can't explain it."

Robert nodded, resolute. "I understand."

He fell back under his sheets and I pulled the comforter over him.

FIFTEEN

A few years here. A decade there. DOD returned after only a few weeks but the aura of fear around him had decreased. The germ he had been cultivating had died, at least I thought so. He still insisted I was hallucinating.

Robert aged, as he should have. At around sixteen, he started looking at Elisa a little differently. By eighteen, she had held back long enough. She told him what she had once told me. They tried to conceal their assignations for the first few weeks, but the house wasn't that big. A father always knows. A father never acknowledges. Robert would hide her under sheets of his bed. He never asked why I suddenly started knocking on his door when I had never done so before. I would intentionally make myself scarce or at least make it easier for them to find seclusion. It was a game I was throwing in their favor.

Kira stopped playing the child around twelve and her aging followed a few years later. She was hoping to enchant a passing fisherman and lure him to the house. She wanted to partake in the same kind of whimsical romance her mother had whispered to her about. But the boats stopped floating by. The cars stopped driving by. I didn't notice it for years.

Elisa and Robert bonded by word of Inari. Ten months later, Eileen Weaver was born. She was normal. A wavy-haired brunette with perky cheeks and a sharp chin. Two years after, they had another daughter. Cassidy Weaver showed no signs of enchantment, though she never cried once. It was their third child three years later, William, that could separate into three wolves. That's three wolves. It couldn't be as simple as Inari. William Junior was formed from three different separate creatures sharing a single mind. They split this single consciousness when separating into animals. One was the intelligent, rational fragment. Another was carnal and libidinous. The third was child-like and inquisitive. Whichever part took the placement at the head controlled the emotional state of the whole while in control. The wolves never strayed more than a few feet from each other and were often seen scampering through the flowers.

Cassidy developed a crush on Guff early in life. Guff asked for my permission to accept her advances. I told him it was her choice but at the time, she was only fourteen and that if he did or said anything questionable to her, I would personally drag him out to shake hands with DOD. Guff decided to wait until an appropriate age.

When Guff and Cassidy followed, I also marked my 76th birthday. DOD never claimed another fairy. Robert never strayed more than a few hundred meters from the property. He never went into town. By this point, the garden had taken up one-half of the entire property, and our food demands were still growing. We were relying more and more on the conventions of the residents to keep the house sustainable. It had been more than forty years since any new fairies arrived. We stopped expecting that to change. Those in this house were the last of a fading fantasy.

To accommodate the growing family of humans, we built an extension on the house, followed shortly after by a renovation of the garage into dual bedrooms.

I would avoid the sitting stone save one day every year. The anniversary of Skye's convention, the day she was allowed to return to land. But she did not arrive, not the next year, not the next decade. On that day, I sat on the stone and remembered her. Occasionally, I heard a disturbance against the waves. I looked towards it but never saw her. Occasionally it was Kira. Occasionally, it was Banya. At odd times, it was actually a normal animal.

*

It was right about that time, as I stared at the empty road, that I told Guff, "I must go back into to town."

"I don't advise it," Guff answered, "what if something is there that will make you remain?"

"I sincerely doubt that," I said as I struggled up from the rocking chair. My mind hadn't faded. Every memory within the house was as sharp as those childhood memories that never leave you. First kiss. First fight. First base. The memories before the house were feeling more like the dream. I couldn't remember what Colin looked like though Skye was vivid like she had left only yesterday.

"There has never been anything out there to tempt you to return. So why now?" Guff asked. His brow dropped upon his eyes, followed by a gaping jaw. "Is something wrong with your health?"

"Every year I push, I'm reminded of how much time I have spent away from her. Like driving from home. Every year I move further from those memories as if I could turn around and return."

"Then what is it?"

I had noticed something that day. It was a small plume of smoke over the south horizon. It was black and heavy. It was how long it burned that caught my attention. Perhaps it was something else. Perhaps my family had been spending more time away from me. I felt isolated upon the upper floor. Robert dealt with his children. Kira kept to the sea. I spent my waking hours with Inari, a kindred spirit I have discovered in these waning years. Guff still visited occasionally.

I was curious to see, to catch a glimpse of the world I was saying goodbye to. Perhaps the end of my life was coming. My body was telling me some part of me was failing. The compulsion was to bid a passing farewell to a forsaken world.

"I just need to check on something," I said.

"You check on a boiling kettle," Guff answered, "on your sleeping child. You don't walk a half-day to check on something. What draws you?"

"Not one car, Guff," I replied. "Not one. Not in all those years. Where are the boats, the people walking by? I just want..."

"To know why?" he finished my thought.

"To know what? That's very different. Don't tell my family. I won't be long." I stood from my chair and started walking. I already had my shoes. I never needed a cane so wasn't going to start now.

"At least have Robert come with you," Guff said.

"No. Leave me to do this."

Guff persisted, following me to the edge of the property. "I believe it a bad idea. I have seen many bad ideas and have whispered words to advise against it. Mine were always financial. So many could have been avoided." I stopped and turned to face the dwarf. "The market crash of '29, the collapse of the Thai Baht in '97." He paused, and then added, "New Coke. I think this is unwise."

"Noted," I answered as I continued to the road.

"As bad as Tudor marrying Howard," Guff shouted from the edge of the violet sea. I spun sharply and offered my confusion.

"What?" I snapped.

"King Henry…1542?"

"Yeah, Ok," I chuckled and continued my way.

"What, too soon?" Guff muttered.

*

DOD followed me from the house. "You will walk away and the government will confiscate an empty house filled with garbage," he said. They'll see your paintings, take in the oddity of it all, and dismiss you as a mentally unstable elderly man."

"I guess I couldn't ask for a more interesting walking companion, DOD," I said.

"You'll be quickly forgotten," he added. I quickened my pace only to see the demon squirm under his limp. The iron cane chipped the worn grey tarmac. How odd that his convention give him an injury. Maybe all his kind had it. He never answered when I asked about it. He just repeated his failing rhetoric.

"How funny that I'm the elderly one," I joked, "yet the immortal demon walks with a limp. Perhaps I should jog."

"Notice how I follow you."

"And I take enjoyment in that."

"Why do I do so, not continue my patrol of the house? They could finally take a moment away from your land. They could run to the rocks, frolic in a loch."

I shook my head. "Why don't we just assume you said everything on that? You gave your compelling argument, like always, and I ignored you, like always. I know your point. You know you made it. You know I won't be swayed. So just enjoy the walk."

Shockingly enough, DOD kept quiet after that. He followed my shadow without a word for the next hour. I kept my attention on the smoke still rising. It had simmered. Firefighters would have tempered such a blaze by now. I hadn't noticed what was in the water until I approached Old Man Storr. I took a moment to pay my respects to the stone sentinel. Ahead was Lock Leathen. The road turned away from the sea at this point. When I shifted my eyes from the rock to the water, I noticed a boat casually sitting half sunk against the shore. It wasn't a fishing trawler. It was over two hundred feet long. In her prime, the ivory cabin upon a charcoal hull could have held hundreds of people.

It hadn't seen a crew in twenty years. Water and wind were peeling the hulk to shreds. It had been driven high upon the rocks. I stepped closer. I could still make out *Hebridean Princess* across its nose.

I glanced back to the rising smoke, then back to the ship. No one had cared to pull the hulk off the rocks, to drag this blemish from a pristine coast. I stepped back, past DOD. I gave him a look. I turned back and made my way to the house.

"You know what you saw," DOD said to my back.

"It doesn't mean anything," I said.

"Yes, it does. The last patch of unspoiled land. You need continue to see the truth."

"No, I don't." I stopped and pointed firmly at the creature. "No...I...don't."

"Aren't you curious?"

"Of course," I replied as I continued my walk home. "That's what defines me. Sometimes I don't need to know the answer. Besides, if the world is dead, you still wouldn't be here."

"I told you. I am a figment of your imagination, the last point of reason you have. And I know you have a responsibility to know and understand what has occurred to the world in your absence."

"Just as I said. No, I don't."

I returned to the house and Guff stood surprised to see me so quickly. "You are not fit enough to be a fast runner, my boy."

I walked past him and entered the house. "I changed my mind," I whispered.

*

My receding hair had left a bleached crown. My cheeks had sunk nearly to my chin. I had trouble reading my books. I couldn't steady my hand to paint anymore. I could feel something in my lungs preventing a full breath. There was nothing I needed to do anymore. I wandered like a ghost through the halls. Ignored by the ordinary people. Hailed by the faeries. I was isolated, kept away from the troubles of the day out of a misguided show of respect. In the real world, a virus or disorder would have taken me by now. I would have broken a vital vessel. I would have forgotten my mind and felt content with vivid memories of happier days. If my life was a record player, then the needle had jumped the last song and pranced across the surface to the end. Now it hopped at the edge, failing to lift the arm and settle back on the seat. It just sat, skipping the last moment repeatedly.

The only one that paid me any mind was my demon. I had finally offered a chess set, placing it on the folding table I kept at the periphery. Every Sunday, Tuesday, and Thursday, we sat across the border and mimicked the actions of players deep in strategy.

"Just admit…you lost," I said.

"I admit nothing," DOD growled as he shifted a pawn.

"I suck at this game and I still beat you every time."

"I was not formed for advance thought."

"Yet you still play," I taunted.

"Because talking leads to questions. Instills doubt."

I laughed and shook my head. I moved a rook to take a knight. "Never cease. Never give up. You're just like them." He shifted a king for no good reason, and I knocked down a bishop in a counterattack. "You know," I continued, "Skye was right. I pity you. You're formed by the division of two worlds. You exist just slightly on this side to give you thought and form. You can't exist on the other side. You came from the friction of two frames of mind, but you sit on one, the same one your convention tells you to destroy. You must be such a tortured soul."

"I need no pity," DOD muttered quietly as he let his queen fall.

"Pity is never needed. It's offered. You think I play these games to humor you. I do it for your sake. Because no one deserves to be alone. And you're of this world, this world, not that one. You don't want to win. You'll never admit it…but you enjoy these moments. You're thrilled I kept defying. You wanted me to win, every time."

DOD opened a small crack of his mouth to growl but only sighed. "You are a fool."

We both knew something neither wanted to say. About my life. About the needle skipping the last moment, soon to find its place.

"I assume you won't go easy on Robert or the others."

DOD finally looked exhausted. "You know I can't."

The game wasn't over but DOD conceded, gently placing down his king.

*

My eyelids unfastened from a shallow sleep. I rolled my head to see the wind-up clock tick five minutes to midnight. It was another anniversary day, nearly forgotten. I stopped remembering my dreams despite trying. I tried to keep a journal but every page was empty. I couldn't manage more than a few hours of sleep a night. I felt a pulling pain in my side whenever I slept on my left-hand side like my lungs were cramping. The mattress was sagging. It would have been nice to have bought a new one before.

Before.

I heard bodies shifting quietly, tolerating my presence, respecting my solitude. I told them that I didn't mind the noise, that I liked the commotion of the house.

I muscled my way from the depression in the center of the bed. I avoided the slippers and walked with bare feet and a cotton robe to the terrace. The breeze was chilly. I grabbed my tattered and weathered black long coat.

I glanced back to the door as I heard someone shuffle in the hallway. Eventually, someone would check up on me. This was not a night where I sleep soundly. I scaled the railing and hoped my age hadn't destroyed my sense of balance. I struggled to throw my legs over. Having succeeded, I lowered onto a ledge of the house. From there, I gripped a batch of plastic siding and scaled down a level. I made a small unsuccessful hop, which I think cracked something.

Away from the house, my sneak turned to a walk. I approached the dark cove. One of the grandchildren had etched something onto the sitting stone with a piece of charcoal. I rolled the black sediment between my fingers. I sat upon the rock and took sight of the moon.

The ocean hadn't changed. The cliffs hadn't either. I knew this was the moment. I could remember her name. I could remember her face. Everything about her was so clear like it had happened yesterday. The moments after and before had felt like an intermission. The curtains opened upon the rock. I didn't feel like a man pushing almost triple digits. I felt like I was still at the sunset of my teens, dreaming of requited love. I imagined looking at the silent brunette in the night club. I wanted to speak up but didn't know what to say. Why did it have to be hard? Why couldn't it be easy? Why did there have to be a game that needed to be played? It had no rules, no conditions for victory.

I imagined waking beside the rock, having lived a lifetime in a moment, rubbing a bruise after falling down the cove. I could return home, find my father alive. Keep the memories of my fantasy by painting every moment I could recall until the last one faded into the dream it was.

If this fantasy had no rules and anything could happen at random, then why did the needle need to be placed back upon its seat? Why couldn't I pull the diamond-tip back to the front, replay those ten years with her? If I could put the arm anywhere back upon the vinyl, where would I place it? I would always choose the first day of those ten years. Even if I couldn't change anything, I would replay it over and over. If there were an afterlife, I would choose that as my heaven.

I imagined burning her coat. She would hold my hand at this moment, enjoying both our final breaths. If she had stayed, we would have had more children. Overflowed the house with life. I wonder how we could have kept it together.

Thinking about it, it never made sense. The house was ample for a family but those that occupied it moved in and out of my life. Where would they go? I didn't remember seeing Philip after I rescued him. I had no idea what happened to Marik the Sitting One. The property was big but not big enough to supply enough food in a garden for all those that required food. How convenient was it for Kareen to arrive, flowing spices from open hands?

My memories of my grandchildren were virtually nonexistent. I knew their names but couldn't recall their faces. Colin had mentioned not seeing the purple flowers when he arrived. And when my house was full, they stopped arriving. As I contemplated the riddle of my life, I noticed a strange shape forming a wake close to shore. It zigzagged lazily in deep water.

I wondered why I would want another life. Why would I desire to be a senile old man in an empty house? What possible reason would there be to want to return to the rock before seeing Skye for the first time? Someone knowing my story would think there was some underlying purpose, some message that needed to be interpreted. Perhaps it was real or perhaps it wasn't. There could have been an argument about perception versus reality hiding somewhere in there. Perhaps the curtain would close with a lingering question never answered. I would leave the last reveal to an empty page.

That would assume there was another option in my life, another version of events presented. Would that not be a cheat, a deception in which I was complicit? This was not some parlor trick. I didn't leave a trail of crumbs to piece together a hidden message. Perhaps there really was a fantasy world. Perhaps magic was a real power with influence over everything we hadn't yet explained. Perhaps in the corners of rooms, between walls, there really did exist these small refuges where our dying dreams sought sanctuary.

Prussian Blue can't cause hallucinations. A person can't age nine decades in a dream pervaded by memories for every year. Skye looked nothing like the brunette in the club. Elisa looked nothing like the blonde. Colin's attention was on the house. He might not have seen the flowers. He didn't notice the giant spinning fan either. Any other connections between the outside world and the fantasy of the house were unintended. There were no patterns, no explanations. This was my life. It might not have made complete sense, but what should one expect?

I stood up from the cove. My toes pushed into the coarse sand. I took a step and let the water lap over my ankles. The coat got heavy with water. I walked further and deeper. It was nearly paralyzing on such withered skin. I forced myself further; each step pulled a sensation from me. My legs went numb. My lungs lost their air. I felt my toes lifting from the sand and I floated clumsily away from the cove. I could hear screams from the house. They knew. They were running to the cove. DOD was watching from the cliff. He lifted a single hand to wave. Good to know he didn't hold a grudge.

The strange shape I noticed earlier was drifting around me. I felt the cold draw out my strength. I coughed a mouthful of salted water once before dipping beneath the surface. In the womb of bitter solitude, I sank until the last bubble floated from my lips. My fingers ran across a furry coat. A flipper formed to human fingers and caressed my neck. I wasn't breathing but I wasn't holding my breath. The moonlight was fading above me as the current pulled me further and deeper from the shore.

A whisker graced my cheek. I thought I was smiling but the cold had removed every other sense from my body. I wasn't even certain I was descending or rising. The light above had faded, or perhaps I had finally gone blind. Something was pulling on me, spinning me around. Then even that sensation faded. I don't remember the sea being this deep so close to shore. I was also fairly certain water had filled my lungs a good minute ago. I was never any good at holding my breath. Shouldn't I be seeing a white light about now? If my life flashed before my eyes, would it finally be the truth I never needed? Recalling a life in its final moments wouldn't waste time by offering dreams. I wasn't evoking a single thought, real or imaginary. Perhaps there was nothing worth remembering. If this was death, it sure was boring.

The pain was gone. It felt like minutes were passing by.

I could sing show tunes in my head. Name every Golden Artist color I had purchased or used. I loved the names given to paint. They were as artistic as the painter using them.

Burnt umber. Cerulean blue. Pyrrole red. I had no idea what those meant. Was Pyrrole some guy that named red after himself? Tastes kind of arrogant, thinking about it. And raw umbar, is there well-done umbar? Cobalt is a gray metal, then why affix it to a shade of blue? Cadmium isn't yellow. I was afraid if I stopped thinking, my soul would drift into fragments.

I clung onto my memories. I could stand to lose working at Home Depot. I could forget painting. My rejections from the lips of real women. I hung onto my selkie. I could have started on the first kiss or when we cuddled on the terrace that first night. Being a guy, I pulled the first time we made love. Then I remembered the second and the third. All the same night. I felt like I was gloating to someone. Like a silent god was waiting for me to acknowledge him. I came this far without needing to explain my life.

I will wake up again. I will open my eyes on the shore as a young man. Skye would be there waiting for me. With no one around to explain away the fantasy, noegic would return. Skye would pull me from depths, having been in suspension for many years. I would walk up the cove and see many houses, spreading into a town. The sea of flowers flooding as an ocean. With no rules to explain how I would die, there would be no reason to. I could quite easily pull the needle to an earlier moment and emerge from the water as a young man. We would never cast out our fantasies again. Skye and I would reenter our home, empty. The other faeries will have retaken a vacant world. Descendants will claim their own patches of land. Skye and I would settle back into our lives, and never worry about conventions, gods, or demons. Without time as our master, we could set the clock at any moment, replay our ten years until infinity runs out.

I still had one sensation left. One nerve was being stimulated. I could still feel that whisker across my cheek. Eventually, even that one faded away, leaving only my last thought before I would awake again.

Was it real?

It only needed to be for me.

Author's Note.

The concept of *House of Skye* came from a dream—A selkie was attempting to find her coat, and I eventually located it in a barrel, realizing then she had placed it there intentionally. In the dream, I never knew her name, but I woke up aware of it.

Moesa.

It was an odd one, prompting a search of my friendly neighborhood internet. One return, duplicated often thanks to Google's algorithm, came back. Moesa is the name of a river that flows through Switzerland. That was not unusual in any way. There was no way I could have known that given that I had never been to Switzerland and had not read up on until that search. When I related this anecdote to friends, they claimed it was uncanny. The idea took root.

House of Skye was the speediest novel I had ever written, barely four months including the research. I decided given that Switzerland was landlocked and had no mythology involving seals, the character's name was unsuitable, and given my love of British mythology, decided to set my story in Scotland, specifically in the Isle of Skye. I couldn't tell you what drove me to set it there, perhaps a search for possible locations for the house, the romantic vistas of Portree, or maybe I just liked the name Skye. I certainly hadn't been there.

You read that correctly—when I wrote *House of Skye*, I hadn't been to the region, not even Scotland. The details expressed came through exhaustive research, including the wonders of Google Maps Street View. I selected the hotels, walked the paths via mouse clicks, and tracking William's journey across the country. It was all guesswork, though I hoped to eventually take my character's journey personally, maybe even stumble upon my dream as William did.

I jest, total skeptic talking; I know dreams are just that. House of Skye was finished in 2010 (I sat on it for a long time), and in 2012, I finally journeyed to the UK. Alas, despite making it all the way to Sterling, and briefly stopping in Glasgow thanks to a mixed-up train path, I never managed to visit any of the book's landmarks. That would be in 2013. By pure chance and bountiful amounts of luck, I had met a girl via online dating.

Yes, yes, you read that right—let's not get hung up on tangential details. It was a single's site dedicating to geek culture and was very successful...obviously. Six months after meeting and three months after expressing affection, I flew across the planet to meet her. She lived in Edinburgh. It was the end of November. Would you believe me if I said it never rained? I woke up to moisture but never got wet.

Whenever you read fiction or watch films recounting romantic journeys where a traveler falls for a local and the pair have a cross-country adventure—an encapsulated harmony where the rest of the world no long matters—you would think as I did that such narratives are complete fabrications, the works of cloying writers creating a fantasy as unbelievable as if there had been dragons in it. But unembellished, this occurred with me. We did have a perfect evanescent romance, one that ended on promising terms, a relationship that utterly collapsed weeks after my return to Canada.

I never said my story had a happy conclusion.

The scar of that loss itch still despite finding local love not long after. I am not one of those people that fall out of love. Those I truly fall for always occupy a portion of my soul regardless of their absence. Those ten days in Edinburgh were dreamlike, with a high point being a road trip we took to Skye. We rented a cheap Honda Jazz, which for the unaware is what happens when you take a 120 horsepower Honda Fit and give it less power. It was like driving a paper-cup. My girlfriend at the time utterly loved *House of Skye*, and part of our journey involved searching for the landscape matching my descriptions where the house might be located.

And we found it; my research proved accurate. The cover of this book was derived from a photo I had taken from Skye, with Old Man Storr visible in the frame. We imagined where the house would be located. As we stood by the road and considered the moment, the sun burst from clouds like an angelic revelation.

The Isle of Skye is truly an amazing location in an amazing country, and that vacation tops my list of locations and experiences still years later. I lament the possible future that was lost despite knowing perfectly well the path I am now on is preferred from any that might have been. You reading this novel is proof of that. But even though I had neither been to Skye when I wrote this novel nor succeed with the girl that would ultimately provide me with the affirmation of my whimsy, I dedicate this novel to both, land and soul.

I made passing comments on my first trip in 2012 that I wished Scotland would adopt me—honorary citizenship. I still await a phone call.

CHRIS DIAS